VANISHED AT KOLOB CANYON

NICHOLE SEVERN

INTRIGUE

To the readers who have to take a break from my suspenseful scenes:
Hold on to your butts.

Recycling programs for this product may not exist in your area.

ISBN-13: 978-1-335-18908-0

Vanished at Kolob Canyon

For questions and comments about the quality of this book, please contact us at CustomerService@Harlequin.com.

Harlequin Enterprises ULC
22 Adelaide St. West, 41st Floor
Toronto, Ontario M5H 4E3, Canada
www.Harlequin.com

HarperCollins Publishers
Macken House, 39/40 Mayor Street Upper,
Dublin 1, D01 C9W8, Ireland
www.HarperCollins.com

Printed in Lithuania

1 2 3 4 5 6 7 8 9 10 LIT 28 27 26 25

"Does taking a case that's possibly connected to my sister's disappearance seem professional to you or what a good agent might do, Agent Perry?"

Maybe she shouldn't be here, but her connection between both victims—personal and professional—held more value than risk in her mind.

"What we had ended when you lost the one thing that could've helped bring Lauren home."

The notebook. Lauren's notebook. It'd been left behind in her vehicle the day of her disappearance. She'd carried it with her everywhere, made notes and sketched out ideas in her pursuit of bringing modern development to the sleepy little tourist town on the other side of the park's entrance. And it'd vanished from Maeve's custody. There in its evidence packaging on her kitchen table one minute and gone the next with no signs of a break-in at the hotel room she'd been staying. That single event had erupted into a series of ripples that had led her to lose everything and everyone she'd ever cared about.

"You owe me this, Maeve."

Nichole Severn writes explosive romantic suspense with strong heroines, heroes who dare challenge them and a hell of a lot of guns. She resides with her very supportive and patient husband, as well as her demon spawn, in Utah. When she's not writing, she's constantly injuring herself running, rock climbing, practicing yoga and snowboarding. She loves hearing from readers through her website, www.nicholesevern.com, and on Facebook at nicholesevern.

Books by Nichole Severn

Harlequin Intrigue

Red Rock Murders

Manhunt in the Narrows
Disappearance at Angel's Landing
Murder at Lava Point
A Drowning in Emerald Pool
Danger in the Backcountry
Vanished at Kolob Canyon

New Mexico Guard Dogs

K-9 Security
K-9 Detection
K-9 Shield
K-9 Guardians
K-9 Confidential
K-9 Justice

Visit the Author Profile page at Harlequin.com.

CAST OF CHARACTERS

Callen Russell—Death wasn't supposed to follow him to Zion National Park, but finding a set of human bones at the base of Kolob Arch may just be the lead this ranger has been looking over a year for. Until he realizes the special agent assigned to the case is one he never wanted to see again.

Maeve Perry—As a special agent, she's confident in the face of death, but a killer's game of hide-and-seek is drawing her close to a past she's desperate to forget. And the ranger who blames her for tearing apart his family is at the center of it all.

Lauren Russell—Callen's sister has been missing for a year. Or is she?

Zion National Park—Two hundred and thirty-two square miles of trails, red rock and danger waiting to happen.

Chapter One

Every day in this place stole a little more of Ranger Callen Russell's soul.

It was funny. People usually escaped to places like Zion National Park and Kolob Canyons National Park to get away, get clarity, find some peace. They took in the towering red rock cliffs, miles of thick, green wilderness and running rivers to find themselves.

He'd only come here to escape.

And it wasn't working.

Nope. Somehow that great big black hole slowly sucking the life out of him hadn't gotten the message that he wanted to be left alone. No matter how many times he'd tried to meditate, focus on his fitness, start a new hobby or commit himself fully to the job, it followed. His sister was still missing. And it seemed nothing—not even tracing her last known steps out here in the middle of nowhere—would change a damn thing.

The muscles in the backs of his thighs burned as he hauled himself up the next incline. He had to admit, it was beautiful out here. Silent like nothing else with barely a whisper of breeze, even in the dead of winter. Vibrant red rock boulders and sheer cliffsides kept their intensity under the thick-clouded gray sky that not even the jagged bare tops of the pines could penetrate. Not many tourists dared to chance the cold, leaving the trail fairly empty. Callen wasn't going to complain about the lack of hikers asking him the same questions over and over. It took everything he had not to roll his eyes and put as much distance between him and the public as possible, but he had a reason for being here. He had to remember that.

There was at least one group out here though. A group of twentysomethings who'd called in the report about finding a set of human bones beneath Kolob Arch.

Probably a prank or a misunderstanding. Thousands of animals roamed the 232 square miles of open desert, wilderness and mountains. The bones could belong to any one of them. Hell, it could be a black bear's lunch, for all he knew. Guess he'd find out soon enough.

Labeled as the largest natural arch in Zion National Park, Kolob Arch attracted millions of visitors every year, with its delicate sandstone bridge spanning from one side of the cliff to the other. But he'd come here for one reason only: Lauren. The past year had gone by too fast, shoving him a little farther away from getting answers every day that passed without any idea of where she'd gone. And breaking his family's heart in the process. His brother, Cieron, couldn't pull himself out of the hole he'd dug since hearing the news of their sister's disappearance. Unemployment, debt, substances Callen had never asked about. He couldn't remember the last time he'd seen his younger brother without those dark patches underneath his eyes, and his parents were just as bad. Sleepless nights, relentless questions from friends and extended family, canceled holidays and family dinners. Colds that spanned months and bouts of depression that no amount of therapy and medication could shake. The stress was eating them alive and aging them decades within the span of a few months, and Callen wasn't sure how much longer they would withstand the not-knowing where their daughter had ended up.

Callen would find out.

He would put this family back together. He'd endure these trails every day and put his life on pause, if that was what finding Lauren required. No matter how long it took.

Low voices broke through the trees blocking off view to the trail ahead, a curve that would reveal the magnificence of the arch and the beautiful backdrop of the red rock cliffs in the next hundred feet. Callen saw the group of three hikers before they noticed him, all younger than his forty years. College age, if he had to guess, two male, one female. "Someone call the rangers?"

All three turned in Callen's direction, each clinging to their backpacks and water bottles with a little less color in their faces. The tallest of the group nodded. "Yeah, man. We…we wanted someone to know. They're just sitting up there. Like someone put them there on purpose."

Dread pooled at the base of Callen's spine. If this wasn't some kind of prank, something had definitely spooked these kids.

Callen motioned toward the base of the arch curving high above their heads. A quick survey of the area didn't reveal anything out of the ordinary, which meant these hikers had most likely explored the oversize boulders stacked almost all the way to the brim of the naturally curved bowl behind the arch. "Can you show me what you found?"

"I'll take you." The female hiker, short and petite compared to her friends, gripped the straps of her backpack until her knuckles turned white. "She's just over here."

Callen moved to follow, leaving her companions on the trail. One looked as though he was about to lose his lunch. The forced deep breaths at this elevation would only make the nausea and any potential dizziness worse. Even out here at ground level, Kolob Canyons and Zion were five thousand feet well above sea level. It took months of exposure and training to fight off elevation sickness, as he'd learned the hard way. "Take a seat before you pass out, and for crying out loud, breathe normally. Your brain isn't used to this much oxygen."

A grumble was all the response he got as both men sat in the dirt, and Callen maneuvered around the first few boulders leading up to the arch after their companion. Despite the overcast clouds, the strands of her slick, dark ponytail seemed to glitter in the muted light. She navigated the boulders like a pro, confident in an I-will-always-leave-you-wanting-more way.

"Just up here." His guide—more girl than woman, now that he got a closer look at her face—carved a path around one of the largest boulders. And pulled up short.

Callen understood why a moment later.

They hadn't been lying. And his former life in private security had not prepared him for this. The remains were clearly human. Smaller than he expected when he'd let himself imagine what he would find. Unholstering his radio, Callen crouched mere feet from where the skeleton's feet protruded in a sitting position. As though the remains had been left here. Compressing the push-to-talk button, he hailed the division head of the law enforcement rangers.

"This is Simpson." The voice on the other end of the channel brooked no small talk or argument. Murray Simpson had a reputation in the park, and Callen could confirm in his study of every ranger contracted in Zion while he searched for Lauren the no-nonsense enforcer solely lived for two things: justice and his fiancée, a ranger in the fire management division. The few times Callen had talked to the law enforcement ranger, Simpson had given him straight answers and offered resources when they were available. It was only recently Callen had dared reveal why he'd come to Zion in the first place, and Simpson had so far kept his word not to spread the news.

"This is Russell. I need you out at Kolob Arch." Callen stared at the shape of the skeleton's jawline, the hole where the nose should have been. The bones hadn't been picked clean as far as he could tell, and an animal wouldn't have left the remains in one piece as far as he knew. These seemed almost...bleached. Too white where the cases he'd studied in which skeletal remains had been left behind were more of a cream color. "I've got a set of remains here. They're human."

Simpson took a beat. "You're sure?"

Callen memorized the curve of the empty eye sockets staring back at him. "It's looking at me right now."

"All right. We're on our way. Until then secure a perimeter of at least ten feet if you can manage, watch where you're stepping and keep your hands off the remains." Simpson signed off.

"Law enforcement rangers are on the way." Standing, Callen held out his hand to corral the female hiker and surveyed the footprints surrounding the body—Was it a body if it was stripped of muscle and flesh?—before backing them up a good five feet where the boulders allowed. At least four distinct treads peppered the area around the remains. Damn it. He'd have to submit his boots to Simpson's team to rule out involvement. Because his gut was telling him the appearance of these bones hadn't been accidental or an animal discarding its dinner. Someone had left them here. "They're going to want to talk to you and your friends before you leave."

The hiker curled both arms around her middle. "I can't believe this happened. Who was she?"

"What makes you think the bones are female?" He carved a physical perimeter into the few inches of red sand with the toe of his boot to mark off the area. It wouldn't do a damn bit of good if a strong wind came through the alcove, but the curve of these cliffs had protected the skeleton from the elements this long.

"These bones are smaller than the average male, and the pelvic bone is much broader, nature's way of preparing the female body for childbirth." The hiker swiped at her face. "I'm studying to be an anthropologist. Gathering data from bones such as gender, age and socioeconomic status is part of the job."

Callen didn't know what to say to that or what to think about the kernel of desperation building in his chest the longer he studied the remains. What kind of man hoped his sister wasn't still alive and suffering at the hands of whoever had abducted her? That she'd found peace like this with a beautiful view? "You can go back to your friends if that makes you more comfortable."

They didn't have to wait long for the law enforcement division to arrive on the scene. One of Simpson's rangers, a woman he hadn't met yet, isolated the three hikers on the trail to get their statements while the man himself stretched out a hand to Callen at the boulder just before the flat area where the body had been found. "Anyone touch the remains?"

"Not while I've been here, but there are a lot of treads inside the perimeter." Callen shook his head as the shame took hold. "Including mine."

"We'll need an imprint of your boots to rule out any involvement." Simpson crouched in front of the skeletal remains. "Agent Perry is taking the lead on this one. Seems this might not be the only victim expected to turn up in Zion."

No. Callen hadn't heard him right. It wasn't possible. "Agent Perry?"

Simpson pointed down the boulder path. "FBI incoming."

But there she was. Every ounce the woman he remembered. And for the first time since he'd stepped onto the trail, cold worked through him at the sight. It'd been a year, but she hadn't changed. He could still feel the sensation of that long, dark hair she'd pulled back between his fingers, recall her wide smile anytime he'd looked her way. Her gasp when he'd gotten down on one knee with a diamond ring in his hand and the one after that when he'd gotten her into bed. No matter how many times he'd tried to forget, she was still there. Haunting him every hour of every day.

Agent Maeve Perry.

Lauren's best friend.

His ex-fiancée.

And the woman who'd compromised the missing person investigation that'd torn apart his family.

Chapter Two

She wasn't going to survive this.

Special Agent Maeve Perry did everything in her power to focus on the remains sitting against the red rock wall as though the victim had merely sat down for a break from hiking and not on the man currently staring at her as though she could burn where she stood.

"Agent Perry, Ranger Russell." Simpson motioned between her and Callen. "He responded to the report and set up the perimeter."

"We've met." Callen didn't say anything more, didn't even seem to breathe, as he turned toward the skeletal remains. Dismissing her altogether.

"Nice to see you again." It'd been one year. Almost to the day. She swallowed the thickness coating the sides of her throat at that last memory of seeing Callen in person. He'd worn that same expression he had now. Nothing had changed in that regard. He still hated her. Still blamed her for what'd happened. And she'd let him. Because it was her fault the investigation into Lauren's disappearance had stalled. She'd been the one to lose track of the one piece of evidence that might've led the FBI to finding her best friend, and she'd paid the price for it. Was still paying the price for it.

But Callen didn't need to know all that. She'd run out of explanations and apologies. There was nothing left to say between them, and nothing she could do to prove how sorry she really was.

Except find Lauren.

She knew the statistics. Lauren had last been seen after a town hall meeting in Springdale after presenting an argument for bringing more development into the tourist town. Witnesses from the meeting itself had stated the meeting hadn't gone in her favor. Places like this, built solely for tourism and to support a national park rather than the citizens themselves, preferred to keep the small town culture they were known for, and Lauren had left that meeting frustrated and upset. Within twelve hours, her vehicle had been located abandoned along the Virgin River, nothing but Lauren's notebook inside. She never went anywhere without that thing, and Maeve had always given her a hard time, but that one piece of evidence had told authorities her best friend hadn't left her vehicle willingly. And Maeve had been the one to misplace it. The chances of bringing Lauren home had lessened every day since, and now it'd been almost a year since the FBI had any kind of lead. The case was dead in the water.

Until now.

Sweat pooled under her arms and at the back of her neck despite the near freezing temperatures closing in. Zion was beautiful in winter, almost desolate and unaltered. The way a national park should be. Apart from the set of bones staring back at her. Maeve lowered herself level with the skeleton's eyeline. Her jeans stretched uncomfortably. Not her usual uniform when working a case, but these were unusual circumstances. “Has anyone moved or touched the remains?”

“My rangers know how to do their jobs.” Ranger Simpson crossed his arms over a broad chest that could probably move a mountain if up for the challenge.

“I believe you. Everyone in my office has heard of the work you and your law enforcement rangers have done in the past year to catch a wide array of violent offenders.” Maeve tugged a set of latex gloves from her jacket pocket and snapped them on before raising the skeleton’s right hand. No fractures or metal pins indicating surgery that might make getting an identity easier. The bones had been stripped of all identifying characteristics, too. Dental was their best bet, but she didn’t have the equipment here. She’d have to have these bones transported to the nearest medical examiner in Hurricane. Maeve moved on to the opposite arm, taking everything in. “Seems to be quite an uptick in crime around here, though. Why is that, do you think?”

“You’re asking why criminals are flocking to Zion?” Callen’s voice cut through the noise in her head, and her stomach bottomed out. There’d been days she couldn’t wait to hear that voice, relied on it to get her through the day. The warmth and tone, the ability it had to soothe even the most brutal cases she worked. But she didn’t feel it now. All that was left felt cold and distant. Hard. “Seems like a question for the criminologists. Not some agent who can’t do her job right.”

Every cell in her body screamed to argue, but she couldn’t. There was no argument, and she’d known coming here would aggravate the no-contact peace they’d sustained since Callen had broken their engagement.

"I miss something?" Simpson's attention pressed between her shoulder blades, but she wouldn't be the one to break professionalism here.

"No." Maeve continued her mental catalog of potential identifiers. While the ME was better suited for the job, there was a desperation building behind her sternum that she couldn't unknot. Something. There had to be something here to clue her in to the connection between Lauren's disappearance and the missing person investigation that'd brought her all the way here to Zion National Park. "Your victim is female."

"We already knew that." Callen shifted his weight between both feet, one of his tells she wished she didn't remember that said a storm was about to erupt. "The female hiker who found her is studying to be an anthropologist. Got anything else that would actually help us, or are you just here to assert jurisdiction?"

Wow. Okay. Maeve shoved herself upright to counter the acid working its way up her throat. Peeling off her gloves, she let herself take him in for the first time since stepping foot onto the scene. His uniform of slacks and a button-down almost failed to contain the amount of muscle he'd put on since she'd seen him last. He was a different man altogether at a glimpse, but familiarity bled through in the details of those intense brown—almost black—eyes and the etched lines at the bridge of his nose. The National Park Service ball cap covering his short, dark hair cast shadows along cut cheekbones and the sharpness of his jawline beneath several weeks' worth of beard growth. He'd never been a beard guy. Never been one to live in the gym, but Maeve couldn't deny the flare spiking in her belly. He'd always been handsome and knew just how to flash that blazing smile that gutted her every time it was thrown her way, but she had the distinct impression he hadn't smiled for a long time. And he looked good apart from the severity in his expression, almost daring her to contradict every nasty thought running through his head as he studied her.

"Based on the lack of deterioration of the bones or any signs of osteoporosis, I would place her age between twenty-five and thirty. A trained radiologist and a physical anthropologist will have a more accurate estimation, but she's fully developed in the ossification centers, which finishes producing bone in the early twenties. There's also the bones that form sutures in her skull. They're closed, indicating full development." Maeve studied the remains, pointing to the skeleton's hips. "The lack of scarring on her pelvic bone suggests she's never borne children, and the texture of the bones indicate she is, in fact, female. Most likely Caucasian, determined by her height and shape of her eye sockets and nasal bone. Her bones don't provide evidence of malnutrition or obesity either, so I would be confident in saying she probably weighed anywhere between one-hundred-and-twenty to one-hundred-and-forty pounds based on a healthy BMI for her height."

A low whistle broke through the hard thud, thud, thud of her heart behind her ears. Ranger Simpson. But Maeve had attention only for Callen. If she didn't know any better, she would say he might've been impressed by her assessment, and a glimmer of hope—of making this right between them—flared bright. Only it didn't last. As though he'd caught himself, that immovable mask he liked to hide behind slammed into place.

She hadn't just lost Callen when Maeve had misplaced that notebook.

She'd lost his parents.

She'd lost his brother, Cieron.

She'd lost an entire future she'd imagined for herself.

She'd lost a family.

The summer barbecues and movie nights in the backyard with their favorite comedies queued up on the projector. Swimming in the Russells' backyard pool or going out to dinner to celebrate birthdays and promotions. Christmas hadn't been the same with Lauren's disappearance, like a vital piece had gone missing. This time of year had always been her favorite—a time for family and friends and a feeling of no longer being an outcast—but she would be spending it alone this year.

Lauren had made her part of the family.

And now that family wanted nothing to do with her.

Maeve stripped off the latex gloves that suddenly seemed too tight, all too aware of the empty feeling on her ring finger. Callen's attention seemed to home in there, too. Like she'd misplaced her engagement ring instead of him demanding it back. "Has the medical examiner already been contacted?"

"They'll be here in about thirty minutes." Simpson set both hands on his hips.

"Great. You'll want to bring in a forensic anthropologist who can confirm or alter my assessment of the bones and collaborate with the ME." There wasn't much more she could do here other than document the scene. Unpocketing her phone, she recorded every angle, close and far, and the area around the body. Several treads interrupted the red sand, but there was something she just couldn't put her finger on. Maeve lowered her phone and glared up into the cloud-covered gray sky. "Does she seem overly white to you? Like the coloring of the bones is off?"

"They've been bleached. You can smell it if you get close enough." Callen maneuvered for the narrow path between two large boulders to head down the rocky incline. "Surprised you didn't pick up on that."

She wouldn't give in to the taunt. Wouldn't break under the massive pressure begging her to air their grievances and move on. Because she wasn't leaving Zion. No matter how hard he pushed. She'd see this through to the end. With or without Callen's help.

Simpson lowered his voice, his jaw ticking just below his ears. "You'll have to excuse Ranger Russell. This case hits a little too close to home for him, is all. He's not normally such an—"

"I'm aware. Like he said, we've met." That wasn't all that hit a little too close to home, but this was an investigation. She would keep her personal life to herself, even if she wanted to scream.

Simpson nodded toward the skeleton. "You think this is connected with your missing person?"

"I'm not sure yet." There were still too many unknowns. Pieces she couldn't put together. She'd been looking for an excuse, she realized. A reason to step into Zion National Park. To confront Callen or to pick up where the FBI had left off in Lauren's investigation, she wasn't sure, but when a witness from one of Maeve's first investigations went missing in the same general area as Lauren Russell, Maeve couldn't sit back and wait. "There are a lot of similarities between Iliana Meyer and these remains, but until your ME has a positive identification, I'll have to focus on going over her movements from the weeks leading up to her disappearance."

"Right. Well, I'm going to be stuck here for the next few hours while the ME takes custody of the body." Simpson rubbed both hands together. "Ranger Jordan can give you a ride back to headquarters. You have the full support of my division. Anything you need, reach out."

"I appreciate that, but I'd like to speak to the hikers who found the body before I go." Maeve was already moving down the path between the boulders Callen had disappeared through. "See if there's anything else they might remember, or if they saw anyone else on the trail today."

Simpson crouched in front of the remains, putting his own assessment together. "Let me know what you find."

Her calves protested the slightest shift in her balance as she hit the bottom of the trail. Maeve sucked in a breath and prepared to face off with the ranger who would do anything to get her out of Zion.

Chapter Three

Too close.

He could smell her perfume. The same one he'd bought her for her birthday three years ago. Something dark and compelling and tied to memories he didn't want to think about. Callen locked his next breath down just so he didn't have to inhale it.

"Sorry. I didn't see you there." Maeve added another few inches between them, literally clearing the air, but some dumb part of him wished she hadn't.

He'd spent weeks picking out that perfume, burning his nostrils and clouding his head before finding the right one. One that intensified her own natural scent and did something funny to his insides every time she wore it. He hadn't been able to help himself, skimming his nose along her throat any time she'd walked in a room. The scent had been as addictive as she was, sinking into the fabric of his clothing and bedding. Following him everywhere he went.

Had she worn it today to torture him? What was she even doing here, of all places? She'd moved to the FBI's Las Vegas office last year. As far as he knew, her jurisdiction ended at the Utah-Nevada border. And the idea she'd specifically responded to this case just because of his attachment to Zion and forced her way back into his life for no other reason than to dig up the past fortified the walls he'd built between him and the time they'd been together.

"You'd think an investigator would be more aware of her surroundings." An oil-slick feeling shot through him at the low blow. He had every reason to voice the words, but there had come a point in the past year when Callen wasn't sure who he was anymore. What kind of man he wanted to be. It wasn't this one. Exhausted, angry, perpetually unfriendly to everyone but the people he cared about. Lauren's disappearance had turned his world upside down, but nobody had warned him how grief changed even the smallest details in his life, more specifically his personality.

Maeve notched her chin higher, and he prepared for the tongue-lashing he deserved. More. He deserved her hatred, her dismissal. He deserved her violence and whatever she deigned to throw his way, and he was ready for it. She cocked her head to one side. "Do you need a snack?"

That…he hadn't expected. The tension drained from his shoulders. "Excuse me?"

"You used to get hypoglycemic after working out and turn all ragey. I'm betting you forgot to bring a snack after trekking all the way out here. It would explain a lot." Driving one hand into her jacket pocket, she produced a purple and clear package and offered it to him. "I brought almonds."

"You brought me a snack." What the hell was happening? Was this some kind of nightmare he couldn't wake up from? Because there was no way in hell Maeve—the woman he'd dumped and vilified for wrecking his sister's case—had thought about his low blood sugar in the middle of an investigation.

"No. Assessing crime scenes can span hours depending on the parties involved, the location, what equipment needs to be brought in. I brought *me* a snack. You just seem to need it more than I do." She tossed it at him, the package colliding with his sternum, before finishing the descent to the main trail. "Hope it helps."

Callen caught the package before it hit the ground. Almonds. He couldn't help but watch her approach the three hikers guarded by Ranger Jordan as though she had all the time in the world. Like someone's bones hadn't been left and displayed for entertainment a mere fifty feet up the trail. Long brown hair had been pulled back, accentuating the perfect curve of her jawline and slender neck. The laugh lines angled from the middle of her nose to the corners of her mouth had seemed deeper, and he couldn't help but wonder who had done that. Who had made her smile when he was still trying to recover from the bomb that had shattered his family? She'd kept herself in shape, lean muscle flexing beneath her tight jeans, and it took more effort than it should have to tear his attention away.

His heartbeat throbbed at both temples, blood draining from his upper body as if gravity had suddenly shifted. He wouldn't give Maeve the satisfaction of predicting his blood sugar had gotten too low. At the same time, without some calories, he'd pass out in the middle of a crime scene. Damn it. He'd expected her to fillet him where he stood. Wanted it. Maybe then he would have a reason to explode, to lessen the fire churning in his gut day in and day out, but she hadn't given him any artillery to work with. She'd kept her professionalism while he could barely hold on to his sanity.

But Lauren hadn't been her sister. She hadn't grown up looking out for her, making sure she ate enough, got to bed on time when their parents worked late or read to her when the monsters crept from the shadows. Maeve hadn't been the one to bandage Lauren's skinned knees when she was learning to ride a bike or hug her if a friend had hurt her feelings. She hadn't been there when some guy broke his sister's heart for the first time in middle school or stood up for her when Lauren's Goth phase took over.

The truth was, he and Maeve might've lost the same person, but Callen's grief was a living thing. Evolving, growing more chaotic the harder he tried to ignore it. And Maeve… She couldn't miss Lauren as much as he did because she just didn't know Lauren as much as he did.

Callen ripped the top of the package open and dumped a handful of nuts into his palm. It'd take a few minutes to pull himself out of dangerous territory. Luckily, he'd—well, Maeve—had caught it just in time. Normally, he'd retreat to his car, where he'd stashed a handful of snacks or pop a piece of candy, but he'd had to hike thirty minutes from the trailhead to get here. Moving down the trail, back the way he'd come, he filled his mouth in one go as Maeve spoke to the hikers who'd found the body.

There wasn't anything left for him to do here. He'd done his job securing a perimeter around the remains, Simpson had gotten his statement, and his low blood sugar was on the rise. The law enforcement division, and apparently the FBI, would take it from there, and he'd go back to his miserable life trying to come up with some other angle he could work in Lauren's disappearance.

"If you remember anything else, or if you find you need to talk to someone about what you've seen today, please don't hesitate to reach out. I know a great trauma therapist in the area." Great. Maeve was wrapping up with the hikers just as he'd started maneuvering around them. She inadvertently stepped into his path, forcing him to pull up short as the hikers continued their venture along the trail. "Sorry. Seems I can't stay out of your way. Go ahead." She motioned him ahead.

The muscles in his jaw ached under the pressure of his back teeth as her scent penetrated his defenses all over again. Was she purposefully putting herself in his path? Trying to get him to hear her out for the hundredth time? It hadn't worked before. It wouldn't work now. Enough of this. "What are you doing here, Maeve?"

"*Here*, here?" She pointed to the ground, then searched up and down the trail. "I'm headed back to my car at the trailhead. This is the right way, isn't it?"

Callen allowed himself a deeper inhale to calm his racing pulse but only managed to torture himself with a fresh hit of her perfume. Of all the days for the constant wind cutting through the canyons to die down, it had to be today. "I mean what are you doing in Zion?"

"You already know the answer to that, Ranger Russell." His official title felt wrong coming out of her mouth after so many years together—intimate years of vacations, sleepless nights between the sheets and planning for their future—but Maeve sure as hell knew how to weaponize it. She was trying for distance between them, a way to keep him at arm's length, and he'd let her, despite the physical vise squeezing him from the inside. "I was called in to consult on reports of skeletal remains. These remains. I'm here to do my job."

Callen swallowed the urge to point out what a stellar job she'd done with Lauren's investigation, but he'd already used up his asshole tokens for the day. Now he was just tired. Of the constant anger, of not getting anywhere close to answers, of hating her when he was still in the habit of seeking her out. How many times had he reached for his phone to send her a text in the past year? How many times had he almost tapped her contact information to hear her voice—even her automated message—when the pressure of keeping his family from falling apart got to be too much? Too many to count. But she'd gotten them into this mess. She'd done this to them. He had to remember that. "News didn't hit headquarters until an hour and a half ago. It takes longer than that to drive from Vegas to Zion, which means you were already in the area."

"All right." Maeve ducked her chin. Anyone who didn't know her would take that as a sign of backing down, but Callen had known this woman since she was seventeen years old, when Lauren had dragged her home one day after school. She'd practically moved into his house, coming over every day, having sleepovers with his sister. Once Maeve Perry had walked into his life, he hadn't wanted to get rid of her, and he had the distinct feeling she was doing it all over again. "You're right. I was already in the area, but not for the reason you think."

"And what do I think?" Problem was, as well as he knew Maeve, she knew him just as well. That was what happened when you fell in love with your sister's best friend. "Because I remember telling you I never wanted to see or talk to you again, yet here you are."

"Wow. It must be exhausting being the center of the universe." Maeve stepped in close, crooking her finger to lower his ear toward her. Her exhale skirted the outer shell of his ear, triggering a rush of goose bumps across his shoulders as she pressed the front of her body and every curve he'd memorized a long time ago against his arm. "I'm not here for you."

That dangerous closed-lipped smile he'd learned meant trouble spread across her face as she backed up a step, and Callen straightened. Hell. She'd known exactly how to get a reaction out of him. Not by attacking with a metaphorical hammer as he had, but with a slim knife meant to slowly let him bleed out. "I'm here for a missing woman connected to one of my past cases. Her name is Iliana Meyer. She hasn't been seen in the three days since her car was found abandoned near the Virgin River, all her belongings still inside, including her phone. Sound familiar?"

Callen couldn't think, couldn't breathe. Turning to face his ex-fiancée, he nearly lost himself to the spiral of messy thoughts threatening to drag him into that dark headspace he'd never quite clawed himself free of. For the first time in a year, he had a potential lead. "A second victim?"

She headed down the trail, her jacket lifting to reveal she wasn't wearing her sidearm. "That's what I'm here to find out."

Chapter Four

She shouldn't have told him.

Shouldn't have given him that glimpse of hope. It was the same flare she'd gotten when she'd heard about the circumstances around Iliana's disappearance and had drawn her back to Zion. What were the chances two women had vanished from their vehicles without a trace—leaving everything behind—within the span of a year?

That kind of hope was infectious. It took over lives and forced people to do drastic things. Callen and his family had already been through so much, but the constant barbs directed at her had finally hit the soft spot beneath her armor. She'd told him the truth. She wasn't here for him, but Maeve couldn't take any more of his hatred either. Not when her body physically ached from being near him. That brush against his arm had triggered a craving she'd barely overcome through willpower alone, and now the ranger refused to leave her side as she commandeered Ranger Simpson's office back at headquarters. He didn't need it. The law enforcement division head would be busy collaborating with the medical examiner for the next couple of hours, and he'd offered his help in any way. That included use of his office.

"Tell me everything." Callen's proximity messed with

her head as she dropped her overnight bag beside the too-small faux-wood desk. He took the seat across from her, that low simmer of anxiety interlocking his fingers, then releasing them. Over and over. It was a tell he didn't allow very many people to see, especially in his work as a former private security operative who'd protected a wide range of clients, but it seemed like he was on the verge of unraveling right in front of her. "Did this missing woman know Lauren?"

"Not that I know of." Bringing him into her case would be a mistake, but leaving him out—when all this could bring them one step closer to bringing his sister home—grated against everything she was as an investigator.

"What the hell does that mean?" His voice sharpened. "Just tell me the truth. Are these two cases connected or not?"

She sighed, wanting to commiserate but needing a professional distance from him at the same time. "I don't know, Callen. It's too early to tell, but there are some similarities." Maeve extracted her laptop from her overnight bag, set it on the desk and brought it to life. Turning the screen to face him across the desk, she opened a photo of the latest victim. "Do you recognize her? Did Lauren ever mention the name Iliana Meyer before she disappeared?"

"No." Callen shook his head, scrubbing one hand down his face as he sat back in his seat. Out of relief he hadn't recognized the victim or something else, she didn't know. "Who is she?"

"Iliana gave testimony in court in my first serial case. She worked as a forensic analyst back in Salt Lake. She was in charge of analyzing and processing trace evidence found at one of the crime scenes three years ago." Maeve had been scared out of her mind to be brought onto such a monumental investigation, but closing that case had ignited her passion for working the next serial crime. Then the next. It'd gotten to a point she'd racked up so many closed cases—some cold for years—that she'd gained the attention of her superiors and been awarded recognition from the director of the FBI himself.

Callen had been so proud of her then—the whole Russell family, really. They'd taken her out to dinner to celebrate, and Callen… He'd proposed that night. Right in front of Lauren, his brother and their parents. Everyone had been so happy for them, she could still feel the ache in her cheeks from smiling so hard. That night had been the first time she realized she'd officially get to be part of the family. No longer an outsider begging for scraps of affection. Though the Russells had never made her feel less than, even knowing where she'd come from. Who her parents had been. After that, she'd done everything in her power to become the go-to investigator her office needed at both Lauren's and Callen's encouragement. She'd come to need their approval and love and acceptance.

Right up until her world had gone up in flames.

"Iliana was reported missing five days ago by her boyfriend. Her phone last pinged off Springdale's cell tower, but the boyfriend can't tell me what she was doing so far from home. Iliana wasn't the kind of person to be impulsive. She ordered the same thing at the same coffee shop every day, showed up for work at the same time, followed a routine when she got home. An impromptu trip to Zion doesn't fit her profile. She doesn't have any debts, her rent is paid up-to-date and she volunteers at the animal shelter near her home on the weekends." Maeve cleared her throat, along with the memories that just didn't want to let go. "The serial case we worked together spanned over a year with more than five victims. Iliana's work and her testimony was the linchpin that got us a conviction."

"And the suspect?" Callen's gaze told her he wanted the easy answer, the one that would point him in a direction and promised to burn the world down on the way there.

"I've already looked into it and the rest of her cases, especially the most recent ones." She tossed a pen onto the surface of the desk. "He's still serving back-to-back sentences for the five victims he butchered. If he has any connection to Iliana's disappearance, he's not making it easy, and nothing has thrown up any red flags from her recent cases."

"I'm going to need a name." The threat of violence blazed in Callen's eyes. This was the private security operative who'd uncovered her past without judgment, who'd collaborated with police to track down her father's killer so she didn't have to, and who'd promised to protect her from every threat—physical and emotional—when he'd gotten down on one knee and asked her to spend the rest of her life with him. He probably hadn't known he would be the biggest threat to her back then. Or that he had the ability to finish breaking her now.

"It won't change anything." She wanted it to. So much. But this was a dead end they would only be wasting time pursuing. "The FBI has gone through his entire life with a fine-tooth comb. While there's a small chance he wanted revenge on Iliana for her part in sending him to prison, no one else from the investigation has been targeted, and there's nothing to tie him to Lauren. I've already checked."

The muscles in his forearms hardened as he leaned his elbows onto his knees, and Maeve couldn't look away. He'd always been handsome, but now? She couldn't take her eyes off him. Couldn't help but wonder whether those arms were as strong as they looked, wonder what it might feel like if she ever had the chance to feel them around her again. "Then why don't you tell me where we start."

The fantasy ended.

"'We'?" He had to be kidding. Informing him about the investigation that'd brought her to Zion was one thing. A part of her felt as though she owed him that much to fix the cracks between them. But bringing him into it was another risk entirely. There were too many variables, some she couldn't even account for right now. Not to mention he wasn't a trained investigator. He had no experience in crime scenes or evidence or protocol in interviewing witnesses and interrogating suspects. "I agreed to share the information I have on a possible connection to Lauren's disappearance. Not bring you in. The park's law enforcement division and Springdale PD are trained to run an investigation like this. You're not."

His answer was more growl than human. "You can't honestly expect me to sit back and let you run this investigation into the ground all over again."

Maeve couldn't stop herself from flinching, as though he'd slapped her, and she hated that she'd given him that much. And there it was. The blame she couldn't move past. Because he wouldn't let her. His parents had called in those weeks after Callen had ended things. His brother had sent messages to make sure she was okay, to let her know he was there for her. Callen's family forgave her, but he couldn't. Wouldn't. She saw that now. It didn't matter if Lauren walked right through that door behind him, she couldn't fix them. She'd promised herself to keep things professional when she'd crossed the border into Zion, but he just wouldn't let it go. He refused to see anything but his grief. Tears she hadn't let fall in months burned in her eyes. "Is this how it's always going to be between us? Is what we had really so far gone we can't even be professional with each other? I'm a good agent, Callen. You know that."

Her heart thundered in the silence in that three feet of distance between them, waiting for him to finally make the killing blow.

And he did. "Does taking a case that's possibly connected to my sister's disappearance seem professional to you or what a good agent might do, Agent Perry?"

She didn't have an answer for that, and Maeve had the feeling he wasn't really looking for one. He'd just wanted to make a point, and maybe he was right. Maybe she shouldn't be here, but her connection between both victims—personal and professional—held more value than risk in her mind.

Callen stood, towering over her. She'd always had to crane her neck back to look up at him, and she'd loved it. His size, his ability to sweep her over his shoulder and toss her around. But this wasn't the man she'd known. A stranger stood in his place. "What we had ended when you lost the one thing that could've helped bring Lauren home."

The notebook. Lauren's notebook. It'd been left behind in her vehicle the day of her disappearance. She'd carried it with her everywhere, made notes and sketched out ideas in her pursuit of bringing modern development to the sleepy little tourist town on the other side of the park's entrance. And it'd vanished from Maeve's custody. There in its evidence packaging on her kitchen table one minute and gone the next, with no signs of a break-in at the hotel room she'd been staying. That single event had kicked off a series of ripples that led her to lose everything and everyone she'd ever cared about.

"You owe me this, Maeve." His voice had softened, providing her the barest glimpse of Lauren's brother. Not the former security expert who'd walked away from the hugely successful company he'd built. Not the ranger who'd fought her on the trail earlier. Just Callen. The man who'd caught Maeve's attention the second she'd stepped into the Russells' house that first time after school as a seventeen-year-old. Who'd given in to his sister's pleas to protect them from invisible killers when the horror movies they rented got to be too much in the middle of the night. Who'd ignored her obvious crush on him and watched her date poor substitutes for years until asking her out for himself. Who'd brought her down to the police station while the man who'd killed her dad was being processed. "Don't put me on the sidelines. Not this time. Please."

She'd missed that man. More than she wanted to admit. They'd spent years flirting, texting, laughing, crying, staying up late to talk and find pleasure in each other, saying I love you. And now they didn't talk.

But this case could change that.

Rolling her lips between her teeth, Maeve bit down. She shut off the urge to ask if his involvement would fix what she'd broken, but she didn't have the guts. She'd brought down a handful of serial offenders and been on the wrong end of a gun too many times to count. But she couldn't survive her heart breaking again. "We start where both of the victims were last seen. We start at the Virgin River."

Chapter Five

He'd been here a dozen times. Maybe more.

The tire treads from Lauren's vehicle were gone now. Police had given up protecting the scene where his sister's car had been found within a couple of weeks of her disappearance. It hadn't mattered much to him at the time. Forensic units had scoured the area for any sign of her and photographed the weeds, sand, river and rocks to within an inch of their lives by the time they were finished. Lauren had disappeared right before Thanksgiving last year, right before winter storms tore through with winds and snow to erase any trace of her presence. It hadn't been practical to keep a unit here just to preserve evidence they couldn't collect.

But there was nothing to suggest she'd ever been here now, and a part of Callen felt…empty as he tracked the white crests.

The river itself wasn't deep, but it spanned at least twenty feet across at this point. The currents had slowed over the past few weeks as most of the rock bed drained, and the snow kept its hold on the cliffs rising up behind the opposite shore. Come spring, he wouldn't even be able to see the smooth rocks that'd taken years of beatings. Nothing but dirt and weeds choked this side of the bank. The section of the river curled along the south side of Springdale but was never meant to act as a parking lot.

He wasn't sure what Lauren had been doing here the night she'd vanished. Whether she'd been meeting someone. Her phone had been left in the passenger seat, along with her notebook, and hadn't given any indication she'd had an appointment or a date. Staring at the damn thing for hours on end after Springdale PD had finished processing it hadn't produced any significant realizations either. His sister was simply gone.

Maeve broke into his peripheral vision, setting him right back in the present. He didn't understand whatever sense he'd developed that cued him in on her proximity, but he could feel it now. That innate pull he couldn't deny. It didn't matter that they hadn't seen each other in over a year—that draw hadn't lessened as she walked the scene end to end.

He hadn't ever seen her like this. He'd gotten the Maeve he'd first put up with as his sister's best friend, then slowly fallen in love with by being drawn into her optimism and sunshine smile. The girl who'd run headfirst into a criminology and criminal justice degree had become the FBI agent who'd brought down a handful of serial killers and faced the violence people inflicted on each other day after day seemingly overnight. But she'd never let that world touch him or their relationship. No matter how many dead ends she and her team encountered, no matter how hard a day or how exhausted she'd gotten from physically chasing a suspect, Maeve had always made an effort to be that sunshine for him.

But the woman crouching in the middle of a long-forgotten crime scene now? She looked nothing like his ex-fiancée. Her eyes had grown colder, the angles of her cheekbones sharper. Rings of black were smudged beneath her eyes, and he caught the first glimpse of how thin she'd let herself become.

Callen's first instinct after hearing the news of his sister's disappearance had been to fix it. To find her. He hadn't been enough to protect Lauren from vanishing in the first place, even with his experience in private security, and so he'd dedicated the past year to getting stronger, faster, more lethal in every way that mattered. Training, honing his nutrition and knife skills, putting in hours at the range, calling in every favor he had with law enforcement friends for details on the case. But all too soon, he'd run out of leads, evidence had been misplaced and the case had gone cold. He had nowhere to focus that training, but he couldn't seem to stop himself. He needed to be Lauren's best option. He needed to bring her home.

And Maeve? She'd just let herself go to waste.

She'd moved on to the next case and the next, putting nearly an entire lifetime of memories with his family behind her as though they'd never happened. Never reaching out to his parents or his brother, never taking responsibility for breaking their hearts. Now she was here, not searching for Lauren but a missing forensic analyst who'd disappeared under the same circumstances. Though he couldn't help but be impressed by her assessment of the skeletal remains. All this time, he'd had an idea of what her job looked like, but witnessing her at work firsthand had shot a spike of pride through him. What that meant for his sister, Callen had no idea, but he wouldn't be forced to sit out this investigation a second time.

He cleared his throat. "Don't most special agents carry their sidearms during an investigation?"

"The National Park Service tends to look down on firearms on federal land, even carried by another Fed." Still crouching, Maeve twisted on her toes, putting her back to him. "And considering your buddy Simpson is going out of his way to help me find Iliana, I figured I should play nice."

Made sense, but he'd seen plenty of Feds carry their weapons into Zion since signing on with the rangers last year. As she'd mentioned, the national park had drawn in an array of violent criminals, each bringing a force of investigators into these lands. Simpson wouldn't have asked her not to carry. "You staying on top of your range hours?"

"Why?" Shoving to stand, Maeve followed a weeded path parallel to the riverbank, picking apart the scene as though she hadn't been here before. But a fresh perspective wasn't going to change Lauren's circumstances. "Worried I might outshoot you?"

His laugh took him by surprise, and some of the tension along his ribs loosened. "That's never been a worry of mine. You forget I'm the one who taught you how to shoot your first gun?"

"No. I haven't, but I can't imagine trail rangers have much need for logging range hours or handling any kind of firearm out here in the middle of nowhere, even with an increase in criminal activity." She pulled up short, sinking to her haunches a second time to move a section of weeds out of the way, and Callen couldn't stop himself from appreciating the perfect fit of her jeans. A familiar, low coil of tension wound him tight from the inside out. Then again, physical attraction had never been their problem. "I wouldn't blame you for being out of practice."

He couldn't help but respond to the challenge in her voice, lowering his into a warning. "I might be a trail ranger now, but I can still put you on your ass, Maeve."

"You're welcome to test that theory at your earliest convenience." Maeve dipped her chin, setting those melted-caramel eyes on him. The promise of a year's worth of frustration, anger and pain flashed in the depths. Then it was gone as she focused on sifting through the weeds again. As though he'd imagined that flare of emotion in the first place. "Why a ranger?"

He snapped himself back from the idea of sweeping her feet out from under her and pinning her into the dirt right here, right now to prove his point. All that lean muscle and soft skin at his mercy. "What?"

"Private security paid well enough. Back home you didn't have to shack up in affordable housing that hasn't seen renovations in thirty years or live with a roommate to survive off your salary. You chose your own hours and worked for yourself." She kicked a rock, overturning it beneath her hiking boots, but kept her gaze firmly down. Callen didn't catch her slip right away. But everything she'd just said pointed to one conclusion: She'd researched him. Knew he'd come to Zion before showing up at the scene that morning. Knew where he lived and about his roommate. Probably more than Callen knew about the man himself, considering they hadn't had more than a handful of conversations since moving in together last year. "Why join NPS as a trail ranger? Was it the uniform? Because I have to admit, I don't hate the view."

Another laugh threatened to escape his control, and for

an instant, he was right back there in the days before his life had turned upside down. Smiling at the dirty memes she texted him through the day and teasing her for the terrible jokes during date night. But Callen caught himself. His smile slipped. That had been a long time ago, and this wasn't a reunion. Damn. It'd been almost entirely too easy to pick up where they'd left off, before things had gone to hell and he'd planned on spending the rest of his life with this woman. The barrier he'd established between them slammed back into place. "I'm sure if you think hard enough, you'll figure it out."

"Oh, we're back to being low-blood-sugar Callen, then, huh?" Maeve moved on to the next section of weeds, and Callen bit back the petulant urge to shove her into the river just to see her reaction. "I think I have a melted granola bar in the car. Happy to let you have it, Mr. Hyde."

Another one of her little reminders that she knew him, that she, out of everyone else in his life, had come to anticipate his needs before he did. But this had nothing to do with his blood sugar. "What exactly are you looking for out here? Police and law enforcement rangers have already been through the area. They photographed and cataloged everything that had to do with Lauren's disappearance."

"I'm not sure yet." She walked another few feet along the bank, then crouched a second time. The weeds were thicker here. It took more force for her to sweep them aside and see through to the cracked, sandy ground hidden in the depths. "Similarities between the two scenes, I guess. Evidence that might not have made it into the initial reports. Remnants investigators might have missed the first time around."

Investigators? The way she said that hit something

Callen couldn't identify. Hadn't she been one of them in both Lauren's and the forensic analyst's cases? She would've already been through here. Several times. "You said Iliana Meyer disappeared under the same circumstances as Lauren. Where was your forensic analyst's vehicle recovered?"

"About ten feet to your left."

Callen pulled up short. "Both vehicles were found along this bank, abandoned by their owners, and police didn't think the cases were related?"

How hadn't he heard about Iliana Meyer's disappearance this close to the park? How hadn't Simpson and his law enforcement rangers connected the two cases together after what Callen had revealed about his sister's disappearance? Was it the time between incidents? A year could change everything in an investigation. Or had the victimology strayed too far to establish a pattern?

"The cars weren't abandoned. The victims were forced to leave them behind." Maeve straightened, turning that intense gaze on him all over again. The humor had drained from her expression. This was the woman who faced serial offenders over and over, and somehow came up for air on the other side. Who'd put herself in a position to face inexplicable grief tying back to her father's murder in her dedication to protect others. And part of him was intrigued by this other side of her, wanted to know more. "Crime scene photos and reports indicate only a single set of footprints was found around both vehicles. Same size, different tread patterns. I'm inclined to believe they belonged to the same perpetrator, but that will be hard to prove unless we have something to identify a suspect. DNA, fingerprints or a note that says, 'Hey, I'm the guy.'"

The police—and Maeve—had kept him at arm's length during Lauren's investigation. This was the first time he'd heard about a detail as small as a single set of footprints. A wave of frustration crested, and Callen found himself closing the distance between them. "You have a working theory as to who's responsible for Lauren's disappearance."

"It's just a theory." Maeve held her ground, but she always had when it came to him. It was one of the things he'd admired about her the most. "But considering there were no signs of either victim being run off the road, a single set of footprints at both scenes and no signs of a struggle, I can't ignore the possibility Lauren and Iliana willingly allowed their attackers to get close."

Callen couldn't breathe. "You think they pulled over."

"Yeah." She brought her gloved hand up between them, holding what looked like a plastic gun with neon yellow accents. "And I think I know why."

Chapter Six

She had one just like it.

The sleek design of the Taser, with its black coloring and small size, had ensured it was easily lost to the thickest section of weeds along the bank. The area itself had been just outside the perimeter police had established upon securing the scene around Iliana Meyer's abandoned vehicle. There was a chance the Taser had nothing to do with the forensic analyst's or Lauren's disappearance, but what were the odds this exact model had been found along the bank? Sliding her thumb along the plastic casing through the evidence bag, Maeve couldn't help but give in to the free-fall of nostalgia.

"It's the same model I gifted Lauren right before she moved to Springdale about five years ago." Callen wrung his hands against the steering wheel as he navigated toward the nearest hotel. They'd walked the riverbank for another two hours before the sun had finally given over to evening and severed their chances of finding anything more. Hours had somehow felt like minutes, and before Maeve had realized it, they'd spent nearly the entire day together. "The company who makes it was one of my security firm's contractors. They wanted us to test them before they hit the market, so I gave them out as Christmas presents that year."

"I remember." The Taser had been Maeve's favorite gift because while it hadn't been thoughtful in the way he knew she collected office supplies she'd never use, Callen had thought about her safety. Hers, his sister's and his mom's. He most likely hadn't put in much effort, but that Christmas had changed everything for her. He'd included her as part of his family whether he knew it or not, and because of that single act, Maeve had realized how much she liked spending time with him. How much she wished he would see her as more than his sister's best friend. Imagined what it might be like to want something…more. "Kind of hard to forget after I accidentally Tasered you right there in front of the Christmas tree testing it out."

His mouth hitched at one corner, though he didn't let it hike any higher. "And to think the FBI trusts you with a sidearm."

"I've had a lot more training since then." She couldn't stop the near wince at the reminder of not having her weapon on her now and directed her attention out the window to the impossibly high cliffs, and she had to crane her neck to catch sight of the first stars breaking through the velvety sky. "Plenty of people carry Tasers. Like you said, Lauren had this same make and model, and I know it's one of your favorites, but we also have to consider whoever abducted Iliana and Lauren may have accidentally left it at the scene."

"You said there were no signs of skid marks leading to either scene and that both victims may have pulled over willingly." The tendons running down his neck flexed and released. "Law enforcement officers have the ability to pull people over. And they carry Tasers."

She tried to breathe through her nose without picking up hints of his earthy pine scent that filled the entire cabin of his truck. She'd spent a lot of time in this passenger seat. It should've been familiar, but all she could focus on was the ache in her muscles from holding herself together over the past few hours. Flipping the Taser over, she made a plan to get the device to the medical examiner who'd taken custody of the skeletal remains that morning to capture fingerprints. Normally, a forensic unit would take the lead in processing the evidence, but backlogs were real. Maeve had the dust and brushes in her overnight bag. All she needed was the equipment capable of reading the print and uploading and comparing it to the federal database. "This model of Taser only holds its charge up to a week, and this one still has a little bit of charge to it. I'm betting it was left around the same time Iliana was taken five days ago. Could still hold the owner's prints."

"All right. Should be easy enough to have them pulled if the weather hasn't compromised the plastic surface." Callen maneuvered the truck into the parking lot of the cute two-story motel, its bright blue doors standing out against beige stucco and brown railing. The motel itself was situated directly outside of Zion's main entrance, close enough that she could walk back if necessary, but far enough away from the congestion of cars waiting to access the park. Pulling into the closest parking spot to the main office, Callen shoved the truck into Park. "I can drop it off to Simpson and his team in the morning, see if there's anything we can use."

There was that word again. We. It pried beneath her hard-scaled intention to keep her distance—physically and emotionally—and wiggled under her skin like a parasite looking for its next host. Her ex-fiancé might consider them a team for now, but she was under no illusion of how quickly that could change. She was no longer part of a *we*, and pretending there was a chance to fix that would only drive her insane. Because even if she managed to bring Lauren home happy, healthy and alive, it wouldn't be enough. She hadn't been enough for him while they were together, and his sister's disappearance had broken him piece by piece. And she wouldn't be enough now.

"No offense, but the FBI has their own way of processing missed evidence, and considering this case is under federal jurisdiction, I'll have my own people run it for prints." Maeve reached for the passenger door, tugging the Taser and her overnight bag out after her and unequivocally ignoring the long blond hair sticking to the edge of her seat. It wasn't the first. She'd already had to peel another three from her jeans and jacket in the short time they'd driven free of the park, and the last she'd checked in the days since Iliana's disappearance, neither Callen nor his roommate were into bleaching their hair. Which meant they'd most likely come from a woman passenger. One who may have been in this vehicle as many times as Maeve had. Had he really moved on so easily? That thought festered until she hardly remembered what they'd been talking about, or that he was waiting for her to get out of the truck. "Thanks for the ride."

"The sign says no vacancy." He pointed through the windshield toward the sign with slim black block lettering beneath the motel's too-whimsical name for being out in the middle of the desert.

"I already have a reservation." Liar. Gripping her overnight bag in one hand and the Taser in the other, she didn't look back as she headed for the main office. The engine rumbled behind her, but she refused to give Callen the satisfaction of seeing her sweat. Because every cell in her body dreaded what came next. Within five minutes of asking the clerk at the front desk to check—and double-check—availability, her worst nightmare had come true. The sign hadn't been lying. Maeve stepped back out into the dark parking lot.

To find Callen hadn't left.

She could pretend to walk to one of these rooms and stand there working a fake key in the door until he drove away. Maybe beg one of the other occupants to let her in for a couple of minutes. But she couldn't fake the exhaustion dragging at her shoulders.

The passenger door popped open, and she caught sight of Callen retreating back behind the wheel. "Get in."

Did she have any other choice? It was either get back in the truck or sleep on the bench tucked near the vending machines. Then again, she might not die from exposure to Southern Utah's November temperatures or a fugitive hiding out in a place like this. The temptation to risk it fizzled in her veins, but Maeve gave in. Heat flared up her neck and into her face as she got back in the truck. "Don't say a word."

"Wasn't going to." He pulled the truck into reverse. "You should know, though, that the only other hotel in town flooded a couple months ago. All three floors are still under renovations."

Of course they were.

"For a tourist town, this place sucks." It took everything she had not to hyperfocus on another strand of bleached blond hair clinging to her knee. Hell, how much hair had this woman lost in one sitting? But the flash of anger wasn't about the hair, was it? It was about the fact that the man she'd planned to build a life with had already started that with someone else. "Just take me back to headquarters. Simpson has a couch in his office."

She could deal with a strained neck and a sore back if it got her out of this truck and away from Callen.

"The office is already closed." His gaze swung her way as he pulled out of the parking lot. "You're not getting in tonight."

"Great." Pinching the bridge of her nose, Maeve leaned back against the headrest. She'd driven up from Las Vegas that morning and immediately met up with Simpson before heading to the crime scene. Since then, all she'd done was fight off the urge to rip Callen's head from his shoulders or brace for his next biting comment. She was tired. She was hungry. And she wanted a bed, damn it. "The homeless shelter, then."

"You're not sleeping in the homeless shelter." Directing the truck east, Callen cut through the short width of town until they reached a winding neighborhood of cookie-cutter homes no one in their right mind would be able to tell the difference between.

The yards, the trim, the stucco, the two trees and clipped grass. They all looked the same. Built quickly and with a few missed corners, the neighborhood played host to an array of off-road-capable vehicles, drought-resistant plants and poor excuses for personalization. Some even with Christmas lights already hung. Because why would temporary residents make an effort?

Maeve sat up straighter. “Oh, hell no. Are you out of your mind?”

“You got any better ideas?” Callen expertly made his way through the neighborhood until they slowed in front of one of the most drab and depressing houses she’d ever seen.

She opened her mouth to reiterate every idea she’d had since leaving the motel.

“A park bench doesn’t count.” He parked in the driveway and reached into the back bench to pull his coat and gear free. “Listen, I know it’s not ideal, but it’s the off-season. My roommate only worked part-time and went home for the winter. So I have an extra room, and this way, you won’t be able to cut me out of the investigation. What you know, I’ll know.”

He had to have been joking. “You do realize we tried living together once before, right?” She grabbed for the door as if intending to barricade herself in the truck. If he couldn’t open it, she wouldn’t have to go in there. She wouldn’t have to be in proximity to him at all. “It didn’t end well.”

“Unless you’re planning to misplace another key piece of evidence during this investigation, we’ll be fine.” Callen got out of the truck and slammed the driver’s-side door behind him. The entire vehicle shook, but it didn’t come close to the tremors threatening to consume her now. He set his sights on her through the windshield. “You’ll freeze in there.”

If she froze, she wouldn’t be able to find Lauren. She couldn’t pay the Russells back for all they’d done for her.

Her fingers somehow managed to work the door handle, and Maeve slid from the truck. Three steps and she was at the front door behind him. Two more and she was taking in the worn furniture, the hint of spice and pine that always seemed to punch her straight in the gut, and the evidence that her ex was capable of living apart from her. Of moving on when she couldn't.

Maeve dropped her bag on the end of the sectional. "Yep. We're going to kill each other."

Chapter Seven

He'd made himself a hostage in his own house.

Callen tracked her movements from the bathroom in the hallway to the second bedroom through his closed door as he lay in bed. Maeve had never been one of those women who indulged in a twenty-seven-step nighttime routine—more like only brushing her teeth as fast as possible to get back to whatever case she was working on—but minutes seemed to stretch into an hour before he registered the final click of her bedroom door.

They hadn't talked much during the short tour he'd given her of the two-bedroom, one-bath two-story and a rushed dinner of Chinese takeout. Almost like they were skirting some kind of explosion, careful not to trigger an invisible trip wire they would never recover from. This… He hadn't expected this. Her being here, in his space, in his life.

Catching hints of her perfume when she shifted on the couch, and the way she bit the inside of her mouth when she was trying to focus on whatever she was reading on her phone, had downshifted his nervous system in a matter of minutes. It felt as though the past year hadn't happened, that they each hadn't lost one of the most important people in their lives, and they were going about their night as they would any other. If he was being honest with himself, he'd felt more at ease during their silent standoff than he had all day. They'd each reached their limit after a day of chasing ghosts and fallen into some kind of truce. Or maybe he just liked having someone in the house again.

He hadn't entirely been honest with her earlier. His roommate had gone home for the offseason, but the part-time ranger had moved out weeks before then. Turned out Callen wasn't what the kind of roommate he'd signed up for. His roommate's words. Not Callen's. Something about his inability to communicate in anything other than growls. All Callen had now was semiregular check-ins with his parents through FaceTime and a dozen unanswered text messages sent to his brother when sleep refused to come. Which was nearly every night, as long as he sat in this purgatory of dead ends and few clues as to where Lauren had vanished.

But Maeve had ignited a tendril of hope finding that Taser at the scene.

He knew the chances it'd play any kind of significance in his sister's case were slim. The device they'd recovered could've belonged to either victim, a hiker may have dropped it on an early-morning run, one of the investigators might've misplaced it during the searches along the bank. Hell, it may have been there long before Iliana Meyer's vehicle had been recovered and had nothing to do with the disappearance of either woman. Except Callen didn't believe any of that. He didn't know how to explain it other than a gut feeling. Because it'd been that specific Taser. The same make and model he'd gifted to his sister before she moved to Springdale. And it'd had a charge left. Not a lot, but enough to convince him it'd been left behind recently. How many times had he walked that scene, leaving empty-handed over and over? How many times had he prayed for something—anything—to stand out and give him the next step? How many favors had he exhausted from his law enforcement friends, the most recent of which had landed him in Zion so he could stick close to a crime scene that'd gone cold a long time ago?

But now, after an entire year of running out of leads, Maeve had shown up and offered him a lifeline.

Callen turned onto his side, staring at the digital clock on his nightstand. Close to midnight. His next shift started in six hours, when most of the world would still be sleeping and no one would be on the trails. Problem was, he was too wound up. Previous experience from holding on to so much tension throughout the day told him sleep wouldn't come for a while. Not as long as she was here.

Flipping onto his other side, he forced his eyes closed. Instantly aware of the creak of the bed coming from the other room. Maeve was an uneasy sleeper. She usually tossed and turned for hours, sometimes waking him in the middle of the night with a backhand to his chest or face or a kick to the shins, until he practically had to pin her to the mattress with his weight and her overactive mind let her settle. Another creak reached through the walls, and he could picture her tossing from her back to her side, to her front and all over again as she tried to get comfortable. It was a ritual, of sorts. Seemed not much had changed in that department, and he couldn't help but wonder if she was restless because someone else had taken over his former duties to help her sleep and she didn't have that now. The bed creaked again. Damn it all. Callen wrapped the ends of his pillow around his head to drown the urge to go lube up the damn bedsprings.

Wouldn't do any good. His awareness of her hadn't shut down just because he'd added a couple of doors between them. He shouldn't have brought her here, but there was no going back now. Scrubbing both hands down his face, he burrowed deeper into his pillows, and the sounds of her tossing quieted long enough that he somehow managed to drift off as he replayed every move she'd made today, every sign of frustration when forced to speak to him. Every time her eyes had grown a little colder after he'd questioned her capabilities to lead this investigation. Hell, he'd been an asshole. More than he'd realized in the moment, but now his accusations, his insults, were all he could hear.

Until those words contorted into screams.

Callen shot upright as his bedroom came into focus. His shoulders rose and fell in big gasps for air. Streetlight penetrated around the edges of his curtains, the clock reading three in the morning. He pressed his hand against his chest. Had it been a nightmare?

A low moan drifted through the thin bedroom door.

"Maeve." His heart galloped out of control as he pressed his thumbprint into the reader on his gun safe and wrapped his hand around the grip of the pistol inside. Within two breaths, he'd ripped through his bedroom door and raised his weapon, clearing the living room and kitchen. The front door was secure. No signs of a break-in at the back door or from any of the windows.

But the screams…

Shoving through the second bedroom door, Callen flipped on the light. And deflated. Curled into a fetal position, she'd kicked her blankets to the floor. Racking sobs shook through her and the bed frame. Damn it. The nightmares. He'd forgotten about the nightmares. Another howl clawed free from her chest, so raw and terrible his stomach seized. He set his pistol on the long dresser tucked against the wall and took that first step.

Then pulled up short.

He shouldn't be in here. They weren't together anymore. He didn't have any right to touch her, nor did he have the inclination to offer her any kind of comfort after what she'd done. But leaving her trapped in that hell, helpless to the memories she had to carry from her dad's murder…

Callen fisted both hands at his sides. Didn't help relieve any of the urgency in his blood. "Maeve."

No sign she'd heard him, lost to her own mind.

"Maeve." He'd been through this cycle enough times before. There was no pulling her out when the dreams got this bad. At least not just by yelling at her. And this one was bad.

She kicked out, her heel colliding with the end of the bed frame. Callen latched one hand around her bare ankle to keep her from hurting herself. Setting his other hand against her shoulder, he willed her to still under his touch. "Come on, Maeve. Wake up."

The full-body flinches and wrenching of her head every few seconds told him she was in too deep. All he could do was be here when she finally surfaced. Skimming his thumb across her bottom lip with one hand, he tracked her pulse with the other. "Come back to me, Maeve."

Careful not to shift her too much, Callen stretched behind her, tucking his arm beneath his head and setting one hand on her hip. The pajamas she'd gone to bed in rode higher up her flat stomach, exposing warm, smooth skin. He drew little circles around her navel, as he had a thousand nights before.

He'd convinced himself tracking down the man who'd butchered her father—a serial offender who'd taken more than ten innocent lives, as far as the police were able to put together—would offer her some kind of closure, but the terror persisted, drove her to the next case and to push herself harder. Sometimes past her limits. Once upon a time, he'd been there to pull her back, but now? Who did she have to remind her she had to eat, that she had to sleep and to make sure she wasn't getting too invested in the victims she sought justice for? And why the hell did he care?

A sigh escaped from between her lips, as if she'd found some kind of release. The worst had passed, but Callen still drew those small circles over her skin. Waited as her breathing evened out and the muscles down her spine relaxed.

He wasn't sure how long he lay there just…absorbing her body heat. Touching her, pulling the last hints of her perfume into his lungs. When was the last time he'd just held still like this? When he'd felt warm? His gaze shifted to the rise and fall of Maeve's shoulder. The answer was right there in front of him, throwing him back to the night before he'd ended their engagement. Before he'd learned she'd compromised Lauren's case. If he'd known that night would've been his last chance to feel this…connection to another person, would he have gone through with the breakup? Would he have kicked her out of their apartment and cut off contact?

Maeve shifted, and he held himself frozen, suddenly aware that he'd crawled into her bed and put his hands on her after everything he'd thrown in her face today. He really was a bastard. "Callen?"

"You had a nightmare." His voice sounded as though it'd been dragged over gravel. He didn't want to think too much on the sensations pooling in his gut at hearing his name on her lips. "You were screaming."

She moved to sit up, but Callen only held on to her tighter. Unwilling for her to break the peace he'd found the past few minutes. "I'm sorry. I didn't mean to wake—"

"You have nothing to apologize for." Removing his hand from her stomach took more effort than he expected as she rolled over to face him.

"You don't… You don't have to stay. I've managed this long without you." Maeve tucked both hands beneath her face. The sight was absolutely ridiculous and completely her, and he couldn't stop the smile tugging at his mouth.

"Have you?" He hadn't meant to ask. And he certainly had no business running the side of his index finger along her jaw. But an unquestionable craving exploded as his hand brushed her collarbone and her pupils expanded to the rims of those dark eyes he thought of so often.

And Callen crushed his mouth to hers.

Chapter Eight

Holy hell. Callen was kissing her.

And she was kissing him back.

A low moan scraped up his throat as Maeve fisted both hands into his T-shirt collar and pulled him flush against her. He claimed her lips as though he'd set out to claim her soul, and the too-small size of the twin bed, the slight locker room odor she couldn't find the source of and the cutting remarks Callen had thrown at her all day faded into the background. There was only him as his lips demanded more and more from her. He tugged on her lower lip, urging her mouth to part, and she gave in. Gave him everything she'd been holding back for the past year. The loneliness, the grief, the sadness of losing not only her best friend but also the man she loved. Losing an entire family. She gave him the nights she'd ordered takeout and ate it alone on the couch in front of the TV. She gave him the empty cold of the other side of the bed and the anger at herself for making such a big mistake that'd cost her everything she cared about.

And he took it. All of it.

A breathless moan escaped her control as his taste immersed her in another life. One where she'd been loved and accepted and wanted. He invaded her stroke after stroke, scalding her from the inside out. And she still wanted more. She wanted all of him again. She wanted him to fill the inky hollowness that'd started spreading the moment she'd moved into an apartment she hated with no one but herself for company.

She wanted Callen.

That hadn't changed. No matter how many times she'd tried to convince herself otherwise, there were some people you couldn't erase on a cellular level. He was that person. The one who'd answered the call after a trigger had paralyzed her in the women's locker room at the gym and she hadn't trusted herself to drive. The one who'd made her a protein shake every morning before she rushed out the door because he knew she wouldn't stop to eat. The one who'd seen past the anger and depression and obsession and nightmares of her father's murder to the woman underneath.

Rolling his weight on top of her, Callen pressed her into the mattress as he had so many times before. Realizing his touch brought comfort, closeness, she hadn't gotten anywhere else. Her legs wrapped around his hips as though they'd always belonged right there. Two pieces of a complicated puzzle. He had his own bedroom, one she was sure was far quieter and definitely less complicated, but he was here. With her. He'd soothed circles into her stomach because he'd known how well it'd worked in the past. He'd offered his warmth because it was one of the few things that settled her ragged nerves after a nightmare she wanted nothing more than to forget. Slanting his mouth over hers, deepening the kiss and his access, he offered her pleasure to take the place of the horror and hopelessness that followed her over the years, and it was working.

For now.

But the truth was, the nightmares would return. Another case would remind her of that brutal night she'd witnessed her only parent die. And Callen would go back to hating her in the morning. Maeve broke the kiss, shaking her head. "I can't… I can't do this."

It wasn't that she didn't want to. She wanted that back—wanted him—more than anything, but not like this. Not until they didn't have this crushing void hanging over their heads.

Confusion deepened the lines between his brows as he stared down at her. He'd braced his forearms on either side of her head, keeping his weight off her, but somehow managed to add a few more inches. Clarity chased back the liquid heat in his gaze, and her entire body went cold as he extracted himself from the bed without a word.

Threading his hands through his hair, Callen collected a handgun she hadn't noticed until then from the dresser where she'd dropped her personal hygiene products. And left.

She stared at the door long after the sun had started its ascent, that persistent heavy feeling of watching him leave knotting tighter as he moved through the house as minimally as possible. Followed by quiet. He'd left, she was sure. Probably for his next shift on the trails, and she…she didn't want to get out of this too-small bed that smelled of men's deodorant and socks. Didn't want to face another day of struggling to remember how to breathe and function as an adult, but Springdale police had already stopped pursuing Lauren's case. And Iliana... Her boyfriend needed her to come home.

Dragging herself free of the sheets, Maeve peeled the bedding from the mattress and tossed it in the washer Callen had shown her in the hallway closet last night. The washer did its job as she found her way into the kitchen and toward the scent of hot coffee. She needed a different place to stay—for a lot of reasons—but getting the Taser they'd recovered from the scene to the medical examiner hit the top of her priority list. Well, that and a shower. She downed her first cup of coffee of the day and loaded her mug into the dishwasher, wincing at the bite of heat against her sensitive bottom lip.

Callen had kissed her. Bitten her. She hadn't registered the pain in the moment, but it refused to relent as she showered, dressed and brushed her teeth. She could still feel his body heat along her spine, feel his weight pressing her into the mattress, his mouth on hers, his tongue memorizing her all over again. It'd all been so familiar and...addicting. The small circles he'd drawn with his fingers had worn a different kind of sensation into her skin around her navel, and a coil of pressure tightened in her belly. Embarrassment flooded up her neck and into her face as she studied the reddened skin along her bottom lip in the mirror above the sink, somehow still swollen.

And now she'd have to walk into the medical examiner's office looking like she'd spent the night being ravaged.

A groan worked up her throat as Maeve grabbed the Taser she'd stashed in her overnight bag and requested a ride share to take her into Hurricane. After twenty minutes of flat desert, cacti and thin swaths of snow, she stepped through the doors of Metland Funeral Home. It wasn't uncommon for small towns like Springdale with fewer than a thousand residents to band together with surrounding cities and unincorporated territories to share a medical examiner's office, but this was the first time she'd visited one located in the basement of a funeral home. *Creepy* didn't come close to describing the prickling sensation at the base of her neck as she descended the stairs.

Shoving through the double steel doors with small window cutouts, Maeve studied the layout of the L-shaped reception area, which opened straight into a wall of freezers and a single examination table that a tall, older man worked over. And the skeletal remains recovered from Kolob Arch. "I take it you're the ME?"

"That I am." The medical examiner craned his neck up without missing a beat in measuring the remains with his gloved hands. The white lab coat did its best to hide the man's exquisitely pressed slacks and button-down shirt. No tie, but based on his clean-shaven face and the obvious time put into his hygiene, Maeve was willing to bet this was a man of discipline in every area of his life. She had to admit, there weren't a lot of medical examiners who could hold her attention in the looks department, especially someone who was probably edging close to his sixties, but this one had a lot going for him. Evidenced by the gold wedding band beneath his latex gloves. "Dr. Yarrow. How can I help you?"

"Maeve Perry." She extended her hand, then realized the mistake she'd made and pulled it back. Nope. She did not want to shake hands with a man who was wrist deep in a dead person. "I'm the agent assigned to work the case for your friend here."

"Well, she's not my friend, but I imagine she belonged to someone." Dr. Yarrow turned away from the exam table, peeling himself out of his gloves before depositing them in the hazardous waste bin in the corner. "I assume you're here for an update on the remains?"

"Yes. I wasn't sure if you've been briefed on the possible connection between two women who've gone missing from the area." She kept her voice as even as possible, but there was no doubt the medical examiner had caught the hike in her tone. "Both of their vehicles were found abandoned along the Virgin River, one last year and the second six days ago."

Dr. Yarrow overexaggerated his nod as he crossed the exam room toward a desk shoved on the other side of the room and took a seat, swinging his legs beneath the cheap metal. "You're talking about the disappearances of Lauren Russell and Iliana Meyer in Springdale. I'm aware. You believe these remains belong to one of them?"

"There are a lot of similarities between the victims. They were both around the same height and weight, both Caucasian, and neither have had children." Maeve refused to show an ounce of surprise that this man had already educated himself in what was probably the biggest investigation a tourist town like Springdale had ever seen. She extracted the evidence bag from her bag. "The police have been through the scenes, but I recovered this Taser along the riverbank. I'm hoping you'd allow me to brush for fingerprints and upload them to the federal database from here."

The medical examiner pulled a paper bag from one of his drawers and dumped out what looked like a homemade sandwich, chips and an orange. His lunch. He didn't waste any time unpacking. "Most federal agencies prefer to process their evidence at the police station. Can't imagine Captain Hendricks would be pleased to learn you're breaking protocol."

"I took one look at the state of their break room and decided I'd rather not have my evidence compromised by grease and leftover spaghetti stains." Maeve hadn't even met Springdale PD's captain, which probably would've been a big red flag if the remains had been found within the town's borders. But they hadn't. They'd been left in Zion, which didn't come with its own forensic lab. Just a sad little wood-paneled office for law enforcement's division head. "Apart from that, I'm not sure the Taser is tied to the investigation. For all I know, a fisherman left it by accident, so I'd rather not get the captain's hopes up until I'm certain."

Dr. Yarrow raised his impossibly blue eyes to her, as though trying to see through her motive. Nodding toward a clean section of counter—closer to the remains—the medical examiner surrendered a part of his exam room. "All right, but you'll have to process the fingerprints yourself. My assistant is on bed rest and due to give birth any day now, and I'll be tied up trying to identify our friend on the table."

Relief crashed through her and nearly knocked her off her very exhausted feet. She was running on little sleep and a head full of questions and self-deprecating criticism for allowing Callen to kiss her. For wanting more than that. But focusing on the case, on what came next, had always succeeded in claiming her focus.

Maeve hiked her duffel bag higher up her shoulder, evidence in hand as she crossed the room to that small section of counter space. Her ex had guilted her into including him in this investigation, but she had no intention of letting him put himself at risk to solve this case. She wouldn't put the Russells through losing another child. And what Callen didn't know wouldn't hurt him. "No problem."

Chapter Nine

He was out of his mind.

And he really couldn't avoid going home anymore.

Callen shoved through the front door, stepping into silence. He hadn't talked to Maeve all day. In fact, he wasn't sure he even had an updated number for her, but he imagined she would've found a way to get ahold of him. Either through his supervisor or through Simpson. Closing the door behind him, he listened for signs she was still in the house. And came up empty.

Warning pooled in his gut. "Maeve?"

No answer.

What had he expected? For her to be here when he got home to soothe the frustrating and alarming need to check in with her? He'd caught himself almost tapping her contact information—whether it was current or not—a dozen times on the trail. He'd managed to control himself every time, but that didn't stop him from wondering whether she'd eaten something before she'd left the house or whether she'd gotten enough sleep. Past experience told him no to both. He knew her. Knew her tendencies to sacrifice herself for her job. And he was being ridiculous. One kiss, and he hadn't been able to stop thinking about her all day. Was he actually disappointed that she hadn't been here when he'd walked through the door?

Hell, he had to stop thinking about that kiss. It'd messed with his head all day, to the point he swore he could still taste the hints of her toothpaste despite brushing his own damn teeth and shoving granola bars and trail mix in his mouth all day. Wasn't possible. Maeve had somehow managed to slip past his defenses while recovering from whatever nightmares had plagued her and wearing that too-thin matching pajama top-and-bottom set that showed off her curves and smelling like her signature amber and vanilla. The combination of her body heat and the feel of her pressed against him had overridden his senses and shoved him right back where he didn't want to be, but could he really blame her? Or was he just looking to justify kissing her?

Didn't matter. It wouldn't happen again. There was obviously a lot they still needed to unpack from the way things had ended in order to move forward in working together, but he wouldn't make the mistake of letting her past his defenses. Not for her contribution in tearing his family apart.

"Get it together." Callen tossed his uniform jacket on the end of the couch, where Maeve had set her belongings last night, and headed for the kitchen. No dishes in the sink. Only a single mug in the dishwasher. She hadn't eaten anything before she'd gone…wherever an FBI special agent went during the day. All right. Maybe she'd grabbed something on the way out the door. But why did he care? He didn't. She was an adult who could take care of herself, and he needed to get a damn grip.

He pulled the leftovers from their silent dinner from

the fridge and opened the first container. Maeve's sweet and sour pork. If he valued his life, he wouldn't eat it. She'd never been the type to share food. Didn't matter if it was Chinese, a bowl of soup or a piece of gum. He'd learned all that the hard way. Then again, what better way to make sure the lines between them stayed crystal clear than to get under her skin? Propped against the counter, Callen ate the first few pieces of pork cold, each bite solidifying in his stomach.

Damn it. It was close to six in the evening. She was probably hungry. Taking the container with him, he headed down the short three-way hallway leading to both bedroom and the bathrooms and knocked on her door. "Maeve, if you're hungry, I've got leftovers..."

The door swung inward. It took him a second to realize what had changed since he'd left for work this morning. The bed had been stripped, the dresser had been cleaned off and there wasn't any sign of the woman who'd shoved her way back into his life. Gravity tugged at his insides. She'd left, probably to the nearest hotel or motel, but what surprised him more was the heavy feeling settling on his shoulders. The same feeling he'd tried to ignore when he'd come home a year ago to find her belongings gone. He'd logically known then what to expect after demanding her engagement ring back and telling her to find a new place to live, but seeing all the empty space where her stuff used to sit, where she'd taken a cold apartment and added warmth with decor and photos and books, had gutted him.

It was easy to figure out why she'd left. It was most likely the same reason he'd avoided coming back to the house for as long as he had. That damn kiss. Scrubbing his free hand down his face, Callen almost ripped the doors to the hallway closet off their hinges. Scents of detergent and humidity had him opening the top-loading washer. She'd washed the bedding. Setting the sweet and sour pork container on the shelf, he switched the damp bedding to the dryer. Maeve wasn't gone. He knew that. She still had a case to work, and there was no way she'd turn her back on seeing this through. What she *would* do? Exclude him from the investigation to avoid a confrontation between them.

"Over my dead body." She wouldn't cut him out. He wouldn't let her. Callen slammed the dryer door a little harder than necessary, then grabbed the Chinese container and tossed it in the garbage. There were only so many places in town where she could go, and considering the hotel was under renovations due to the flood, she would've gone back to the motel that'd been full last night.

He crossed the living room to collect his jacket from the sectional. His phone vibrated in his back pocket. Pulling it free, Callen lost every ounce of frustration in a rush, leaving him more than a little disoriented. He connected the call. "Hey, Mom."

His mother's face filled the screen, a little off-center and too low to get a full view of anything other than the top of her fully white, slicked, straight hair. "Hello, darling. I thought you were going to call last night."

"Yeah. I'm sorry. Something came up." Rather, some*one*, but his parents didn't need to know about Maeve. "I sent a text letting you know I wasn't going to make it. Did you see it?"

"Is that Callen?" His father's gravelly voice registered a split second before the old man himself pushed his way into the frame. Stark lines puddled beneath his dad's eyes, as though age was dragging all the skin in the man's face down. His beard and mustache—normally kept neat and short—had gone gray like he'd been electrocuted repeatedly over the last year, but Callen had felt that too. The shock of grief anytime Lauren crossed his mind. He couldn't imagine what it was like losing a child. Losing a sister was bad enough. "You finish reading that book I told you about? What'd you think of the ending? Crazy, huh? The killer was right there in front of you the whole time—"

"Oh, stop, Tommy. I haven't gotten that far. You're going to spoil it for me." Helen Russell's laugh didn't reach her eyes as she slapped her husband's arm. There'd been years Callen remembered when that hadn't been the case, but their monthly family book club—and time—had started bringing the smile he remembered back. Cieron was the only one who didn't show, didn't call, didn't seem to want anything to do with the family.

Leaving Callen to shoulder the weight alone.

"I'm just teasing." His dad leaned in and planted a kiss on his mom's forehead. "The killer is—"

"Utter one more syllable and you're sleeping on the couch tonight." Turned out, his mother's "mom voice," as she liked to call it, was just as effective on a doting husband, shutting Tommy Russell up in an instant.

Callen couldn't stop the laugh from charging up his throat. Moments like this had made more of an appearance over the past few months. Where he'd gotten glimpses of life before Lauren had gone missing. More were on the horizon each week he checked in, but they would never outshine the darkness as long as his sister's case remained open. Until then, he'd protect the ones left with everything he had.

"How's your week, honey? Anything exciting going on in Zion?" His mother clapped both hands together, her lipsticked mouth parting. "Oh, that reminds me, did Maeve get ahold of you? I keep forgetting to ask."

"Maeve?" Callen didn't understand. His hand gripped the sides of the phone until his case protested. "What are you talking about? You've been talking with Maeve?"

"Well, we've stayed in touch since you broke up. I told you that. She calls every couple of weeks to check on us, and she sent us that framed photo of you, Cieron and Lauren for Christmas last year. You know, the one on the bookcase.

"Last time I talked to her, she was headed to Zion. I told her to call you."

"You've stayed in touch with my ex." The words made sense as they left his mouth, but Callen couldn't wrap his head around the meaning. His next exhale faltered. He remembered the photo. It'd been taken the same year he'd gifted Lauren, Maeve and his mom the Tasers. Maeve had been the one to take it. For once, all three Russell children in the same house, and his mom had wanted an updated photo to replace the one of them as teens almost two decades prior, but he hadn't thought much about how it'd shown up on the bookcase. "For a year."

"You say that like she stopped existing after you broke up with her." The mom voice was back, directed at him, and Callen couldn't stop every nerve ending in his body screaming for him to hang up before he dug his own grave. "Do I have to remind you, Maeve has been part of this family since she was seventeen years old? She isn't just Lauren's best friend. She's like another daughter to me. She was going to be my daughter after you got married, and she's done nothing but try to make things right since Lauren disappeared. If it weren't for her, your father and I wouldn't be able to laugh with you today."

Tommy Russell lost the playfulness in his expression. "She made a mistake, boy. We know that, she knows that. But we've forgiven her. You have no idea how bad things got after you broke off the engagement. She didn't have anyone."

"Wait. Back up. You said you talked with her a couple weeks ago, and she told you she was coming to Zion?" Callen couldn't think straight. Maeve had been talking with his parents, and they'd forgiven her? How bad had things gotten for his parents to get to that point? Heat exploded from that hollow place in his chest. None of this made sense. How had Maeve known to come to Zion before Iliana Meyer had disappeared?

His mom nodded, strands of her white hair sliding free from one shoulder. "Yes. She said she needed to start at the beginning."

He didn't understand. Maeve had been in Springdale and Zion for weeks rather than just the past two days? Why hadn't she told him? Why come here at all? It couldn't have been to look into Iliana Meyer's disappearance. The forensic analyst's vehicle hadn't been found until six days ago. Callen ran through everything, every conversation, every move made on Maeve's part since showing up at the scene of the skeletal remains yesterday morning. "The beginning of what?"

"Of Lauren's case. Didn't she tell you?" Helen Russell finally centered herself on the screen. "She's still looking into your sister's disappearance."

Chapter Ten

The federal database was lying.

Maeve scoured the report for the hundredth time, but the information printed on the single sheet of paper hadn't changed. She'd gotten two clean fingerprints off the Taser's casing, with a few more partials that'd been smudged or eroded by weather, wildlife or location. A one hundred percent match.

It wasn't possible. It couldn't be possible. But no matter how many times she blinked, the data didn't lie.

A knock sounded at the room's only door, racketing her heart rate higher. She'd hung the Do Not Disturb sign on the handle, and the housekeepers had already been through when they'd gotten the room ready. Who else knew she was here?

Maeve slipped the fingerprint results under her laptop. She'd lucked out when she stopped by the motel last night after processing the fingerprints in the medical examiner's office: One room available. She'd snatched it up without even asking the nightly rate, not ready to face Callen after what had happened last night.

That kiss. She'd thought about it all damn day when her brain wasn't trying to convince Dr. Yarrow she wasn't some random stranger off the street trying to get access to his morgue. Her credentials helped, but there'd still been a few suspicious looks thrown her way as she'd dusted the Taser on the small space of countertop he'd granted her. Ugh. Why did Callen have to kiss her? She'd gone an entire year without remembering what his mouth had felt like on hers, and he'd blown it up in one single night.

Furnished with a queen-size bed, a dresser, two nightstands, a desk and a bathroom, the room provided space for her to work and get her head on straight. Two-for-one special. All the floral prints on the curtains, wallpaper and bedding were beginning to give her a headache, though.

Another knock sounded, and she crossed the small distance from the desk. Maeve wrenched open the heavy door. "What about Do Not Disturb do you not under—"

Crap.

Her brain short-circuited at the sight of the man staring down at her. "What are you doing here? How did you find me?"

"We need to talk." Callen crossed the threshold, and maybe a part of her had let him. While he was definitely not an opponent she'd want to face in the ring or the field, between his foundational training and the FBI's close-quarters combat instruction, she could hold her own.

Maeve closed the door behind him, and the space she'd appreciated a few minutes ago suddenly seemed so much smaller with him taking up a big portion of it. "All right. Start by answering my question. How did you know I was here?"

"Where else would you have gone?" Callen surveyed the room, most likely memorizing the layout like he'd taught her when she was a seventeen-year-old, paranoid her father's killer would come back for her. He took a step toward her open laptop. "Would've appreciated a heads-up, though. I wouldn't have felt so bad about eating your sweet and sour pork from last night."

Darting to head him off, Maeve slammed her computer closed. She had other notes—handwritten and piled together—he could riffle through, but she got the impression he wasn't here about her investigation. She crossed her arms over her breasts, wishing she hadn't changed into her tank top and sweats. "We both knew me staying with you was temporary. As for the pork, I left it for you."

"Liar. You're more territorial about food than a pack of wolves." He didn't seem to know what to do with himself: take a seat at the desk or on the edge of the bed. "And I'm sure you're already thinking of ways to make me pay for eating it."

She'd already thought of three, but she wasn't going to tell him that. They would be a surprise. "Is there an actual reason you're here, or did you come all this way to experience my sparkling personality?"

"You've been staying in touch with my parents." Settling dark eyes on her, Callen took a step toward her. All muscle and spice and dark hair curling at the nape of his neck. "My mom told me you and them have been talking every couple of weeks since we broke up. That you have been checking in on them and helping them get through their grief. Making appointments for them with a therapist you knew and sending them Christmas presents and birthday cards and flowers for their anniversary. Why?"

That…was not what she'd expected out of his mouth. Her throat dried up, but she wouldn't let him corner her. "What do you mean?"

"I mean why would you do that?" His hair stuck up

at the front as though he'd run his hands through it over and over. He probably had. It was one of the things she'd liked to tease him about when he was stressed at work. Usually, that teasing had turned his attention on her, and they'd distract each other for a while. Not anymore. "Why would you do that for my parents after everything that happened?"

Was he serious? Helen and Tommy Russell weren't just his parents. They'd had a hand in making sure she was fed, that she had a roof over her head when the bank had taken the house because she didn't know how to pay the mortgage, made sure she didn't have to sit alone at the funeral and tried to help her track down her mother. That last one had been in vain, but they'd been there when her father couldn't be, and she owed them. More than they knew. He knew that. He knew all that, and he was standing there asking why she'd tried to step in to make sure they didn't unravel into depression or worse? "I thought you knew. That we were in contact."

"You..." His shoulder rose on a deep inhale, and she couldn't help but appreciate the work he'd put into the muscle stretching his uniform despite her desperate need to avoid him altogether. "You didn't have to do that. They're my parents. It was my job to get them through losing Lauren, and I... I obviously failed, if they couldn't even tell me they were going to therapy at your insistence."

Emotion she didn't want to name clogged her throat. "You didn't fail. You're right. Helen and Tommy are your parents, and I'm sorry if I crossed the line and that you're only learning about this now, but I owe them a lot. They took me in after my dad died. I couldn't just turn my back on them after you and I broke up."

"Thank you." Callen stepped closer, eliciting a shiver and pimpling goose bumps along her arms. "For helping them."

He was too close again. Too warm and big and inviting. Her head spun with a thousand different outcomes of this single interaction, none of which would end well. He'd ended things between them. He hated her for the mistake she'd made. He'd given up on them, and what? Now he had no problem kissing her? Touching her? Maeve stepped out of his reach, maneuvering around him back toward the desk. She stacked her notes in a hurry, earning a paper cut in the process. "You don't need to thank me."

"But I am. They told me how big of an influence you've been in getting them through this." His voice seemed to follow her, skimming along her exposed skin and settling low in her belly. Callen dragged a hand across her low back, and every nerve she owned fired in response, urged her to lean back just enough to plaster herself to his body. "They also said they've forgiven you for what happened during Lauren's investigation."

Her spine stiffened, and Maeve forgot what she was doing with her hands. She didn't know what to say to that, what to think. Because while she was grateful his parents had come so far, it wasn't their forgiveness she needed. "But do *you*?"

Pressure built beneath her sternum as she waited for his answer. And waited. The silence took physical form as Callen stepped back, dragging his fingers along her hips, and put some much-needed distance between them.

She already knew the answer, and for some reason, that hurt more than him ending their engagement.

She pulled the fingerprint results from beneath her laptop, still at a loss in identifying the last person to touch that Taser. And off-balance from the loss of warmth of his hands tunneling through her tank top. She wouldn't think about that. How much she'd missed touching him, breathing in that infuriating scent of his. How she'd missed his habit of reaching out whenever they were in the same room together. It didn't matter where they were, who they were with, his impulse to tangle his fingers in her hair or press his arm against hers, to slide his hand along her lower back or knock his knee into hers beneath a table had always triggered a feeling of being wanted. Needed.

And she hadn't felt that in a long time. Wanted by him. By anyone. The case. That was all that mattered. Because there were two women out there who needed her help. Turning into him, she clutched the fingerprint results as she settled back against the edge of the desk. "There's something I need to talk to you about."

Callen slid his thumb along his bottom lip. "I already know you've been working Lauren's case all this time."

Her lips parted, but it didn't take long for her to put the pieces together. She nodded, folding her arms across her midsection. It didn't do a damn bit of good to relieve the tension in the air, but it offered her a minuscule amount of protection. "Your mom told you I came here a couple weeks ago. Not yesterday, like I led you to believe."

"Why wouldn't you tell me?" He sank back onto the edge of her bed where she'd tossed her overnight bag and pretty much everything she owned at this point in her life. "I've been searching for a lead for over a year with nothing to show for it. You should've involved me the moment you set foot in Zion. I deserved to know."

"You can't seriously be asking that question." Her defenses were shuttering into place, hiking her voice higher, pumping her blood harder. There wasn't any physical threat, but her brain couldn't tell the difference, screaming for her to get the hell as far from Callen as she could manage. "What about when you said you didn't ever want to see or hear from me again after I admitted to mishandling evidence in the investigation? Does that ring a bell?"

He set his elbows on his knees, that gaze drilling through her. "That doesn't have anything to do with you working the case now."

"Doesn't it?" She nearly crumpled the paper in her hand as her emotions got the better of her. This wasn't about the case. This wasn't about his parents or the fact that she'd misled him. This was a complete desolation of the wall under which she'd buried her hurt and rejection. "You threw me out of your life like I was nothing to you—like everything we shared and promised each other was nothing—and now you're asking why I didn't tell you I was in town or that I've been working your sister's investigation? Do you understand how confusing it was when you kissed me last night? How it feels to wake up to you in my bed or with your hands on me with those words still in my head?"

The color drained from his face, and Callen leaned back, as though welcoming the reality check. "You weren't nothing, Maeve."

She wished she believed that, but his actions had shown her different. "You know what? It doesn't matter. Like I said before, I'm not here for you. I'm here to find the connection between two missing women and do whatever it takes to bring them home." Closing the distance between them, she shoved the fingerprint results into his chest. "Now, tell me how the hell your fingerprints ended up on that Taser we recovered from the scene."

Chapter Eleven

He had no idea what he was looking at.

The words on the page spelled it out easily enough, but he couldn't process what Maeve was saying. "I don't understand."

"What about the results don't you understand?" She dropped her hands to her sides, the picture of *relaxed*, but Callen knew what kind of fighter she'd become. "The Taser we recovered isn't just the same make and model as the ones your private security firm used in the field or the ones you gifted to the women in your family that Christmas. According to this, it's yours."

That…wasn't possible.

His head had started spinning the moment she accused him of believing what they'd had together as a couple meant nothing, but now Callen was on the verge of losing it altogether. One of his Tasers had shown up at the crime scene of a missing forensic analyst and his sister.

"I took the Taser to the medical examiner's office. I printed the device and uploaded the prints to the federal database myself." Maeve was pacing now—or trying to get closer to wherever she'd stashed a weapon, he wasn't sure yet. "Why was it at the scene, Callen? What aren't you telling me?"

Callen shook his head, still staring at the data in front of him. She had to ask these questions, he knew that, and based on their conversation a couple minutes ago, she had every reason not to trust the words out of his mouth, but there was no chance in hell this investigation linked back to him. He handed back the results. “It’s not mine.”

Her laugh told him how much she took him at his word. “The fingerprints—”

“Could’ve been planted there by anyone.” Shoving to his feet, he threaded his hand through his hair. Hell, he’d had every intention of confronting Maeve about working Lauren’s case without bringing him in sooner and had somehow ended up the most likely suspect in a forensic analyst’s disappearance. He didn’t even know Iliana Meyer. They’d never crossed paths, as far as he knew, but he came face-to-face with hundreds of hikers on the trails this time of year. Was it possible she’d been one of them? “Yes, it’s the same make and model of the Taser I own, but I’m telling you right now, it’s not mine. All of my gear—my weapons, my ammunition, my tactical supplies—are locked up in a storage unit.”

That seemed to get her attention. Narrowing her gaze on him, Maeve stopped her pacing, her shoulders pulling back. “What storage unit?”

“It’s a self-storage place in town. They use shipping containers secured by padlocks. I’m the only one with a key to my unit.” Though he had to admit, it’d been a while since he’d visited the storage unit. There hadn’t been any need. But how else could one of his Tasers, with his fingerprints, end up at the scene? “I couldn’t off-load that much gear and weaponry before relocating to Springdale, and my roommate wasn't comfortable living in an armory, so I got the storage unit. I can take you there."

Maeve was already on the move, bypassing him in favor of the black overnight bag on her bed. She extracted a shirt and headed for the attached bathroom. The door swung shut but didn't close all the way, drawing his attention to the backlit movement through the crack. After drawing her tank top over her head, she discarded it somewhere on the floor, exposing her bare back, and Callen sucked in a shallow breath. "Did the storage facility supply the lock, or were you required to provide your own?"

"I bought my own. A closed-shackle padlock. Makes it nearly impossible for someone to use a saw or bolt cutters to get inside without the key." He tracked the flex and release of the muscles down her back through the crack in the door no bigger than an inch wide, unable to take his eyes off her. The smooth skin down her spine, the mole he'd kissed a thousand times over the back of her left hip, the tattoo detailing her father's birth and death dates along one shoulder. Heat simmered low in his gut, and Callen forced himself to break the spell as she pulled one of her workout bras into place, followed by her shirt.

Yep. He was going to hell. Because she'd been right before. Climbing into her bed last night, the kiss, this uncontrollable need to keep her within arm's reach—none of it had anything to do with the investigation and everything to do with whatever closure he hadn't gotten from ending things between them. He'd slipped back into habits that no longer served either of them and were only working to screw with their heads.

The door to the bathroom flew open, basking Maeve in yellowish light that did nothing to deter from her beauty as she tossed her tank top on the bed beside him. "Does anyone else have access to the storage container?"

"No. Just me." A low buzz started in his head as her arm brushed against his in an effort to pull on a pair of socks and her tennis shoes.

The outfit she'd chosen was a combination of sweats and what looked to be one of her work shirts, but she pulled it off by throwing her long hair into a ponytail. "And the payments are up-to-date? There's no chance the facility decided to auction off your armory?"

"Up-to-date and on time every month." Between that storage unit, his cell phone bill, groceries and his rent, he didn't have much else to spend his money on. The funds would be there if something had come up, and he hadn't gotten notice from his personal security system that the unit had been tampered with. "I'm telling you, the Taser isn't mine. Something else is going on here."

Maeve stilled. "All right. Then who would want to put your fingerprints at that scene, and how would they know about your preferred Taser?"

That was a good question. The list of suspects had shortened over the past year as he'd dived into every aspect of Lauren's life. From the frustrated city councilman who'd shut down his sister's proposal for development expansion to the local artist boyfriend whom Lauren had promised to commission for her latest project and the landowner who'd refused to sell his property for a new batch of town houses—neither he nor the investigators had found motive for Lauren's disappearance. Background checks, surveillance, financial inquiries. Nothing had raised a red flag. "I don't know."

She seemed to consider his words, her jaw loosening and tightening. "Then let's find out."

Within five minutes, they were on the road. Another twenty and Callen pulled his truck into the blockaded storage facility entrance and punched in the six-digit code into the keypad for after-hours access. Twelve-foot cinder block walls and a closed-circuit surveillance system acted as deterrents for criminals, but Callen had no other way to explain how a Taser with his fingerprints had ended up at a crime scene.

"Are entry codes individual to each storage owner?" Maeve's attention burned into him from the passenger seat as the gates slowly receded to one side of the lot. She was tense as she picked at her clothes on the way over, and he couldn't help but be reminded that they hadn't finished their earlier conversation.

He could already see where she was headed with this lead, though. An individual code would allow them to track who'd entered the property. Unfortunately, that wasn't how this place operated. He pressed on the accelerator, turning right toward his unit. The shipping containers weren't in any real kind of order, as they'd been shuffled over the years, but his was easily accessible compared to some others. He'd made sure of it. "One code for everybody."

"And you chose this place?" She scanned the layout of the units as though she needed to make a quick escape. "Would've thought you'd be a little more security minded than that."

"I have my own security system up and running in the container." Problem was, there were times the unit got too hot under the blazing Southern Utah sun. No system was perfect, and his had shorted out this past summer, at least three times that he was aware of.

"That sounds more like it." She seemed to be looking everywhere but at him, the tightness in her shoulders more exaggerated under the spotlights installed outside every other unit.

"About last night." Callen pulled up in front of his assigned shipping container and shoved the truck into Park but didn't move to get out. "I shouldn't have kissed you. I just… I got caught up in the familiarity of the whole situation, and I didn't want you to wake up alone. I know it's not my place anymore, and I'm sorry."

Her throat worked on a strong swallow. "It helped."

He knew that from years of firsthand experience. Once they'd finally gotten past their own reservations about dating and how it would affect Lauren, there hadn't been more than a handful of days in the five years they were together that didn't end with one of them in the other's bed. Nights where no matter how hard he tried, he couldn't fight those terrors for her. "It won't happen again."

"I'm sure the guests of Days Inn will be very disappointed to hear that." Her smile triggered a raise of his mouth. Hell, she'd never smiled enough. There'd been entire weeks—now close to a year—where he'd gone without it, and that hit to his system rocketed him into a near high. "But your girlfriend will probably be relieved."

Confusion doused his weightlessness. Callen didn't even register how hard he'd been clutching the steering wheel until his knuckles hurt. "Girlfriend?"

"The one who owns all these hairs sticking to my clothes." She picked at something on the seat and dragged it into the dim light of the control panel. A single long blond hair. "You could make an entire new woman out of how much she's left in my seat alone. Can't imagine what the back bench looks like, knowing your preference for truck sex."

Callen couldn't stop the laugh that burst from his chest. "Is that why you've been so tense since you got in the truck? You think I'm seeing someone? And, what? I cheated on them last night by kissing you?"

"Did you?" She flung the hair out of sight near her feet as though she couldn't stand to be in the same vehicle as it, let alone have it touch her.

"The hair belongs to my former roommate. He didn't believe in owning his own car, so I drove him to run errands and carpool to work. A lot. So believe me when I tell you, you won't find his hair in the back seat." At least, he hoped not. "But it's good to know your feelings on whether or not I'm dating."

"You're an ass." Shoving free from the truck cab, Maeve slammed the door behind her before rounding the hood of the vehicle, the headlights casting her shadow against the storage container as she inspected the padlock.

She'd cared. About whether or not he'd moved on. The idea had gotten to her, but hadn't it done the same to him last night? When he'd wondered whether she had someone waiting for her back in Vegas who helped with her nightmares?

Callen cut the engine and climbed out after her, padlock key in hand. He shouldn't care what was going on in her life or whether she'd found someone to warm her bed. They weren't together anymore. They were barely acquaintances at this point. But just like that kiss, he couldn't stop thinking about who she might have been with since she'd left. If they knew her favorite junk food was popcorn with Junior Mints, or that she needed three ibuprofen and to watch *The Office* while on her period. Did she smile for them? Did they make her happy?

Hands on her hips, Maeve turned to face him, not even the spotlights able to take away from the intensity in her gaze. "I take it you haven't been out here in a while."

"Few weeks." He separated the padlock key from the rest on his key ring as he approached the door. "Why?"

"Because your padlock is broken." She pointed to the unit. "Someone out there got complete access to your armory."

Chapter Twelve

Maeve rushed for the door, discarding the severed padlock and pulling at the heavy metal. Fluorescent lights she was sure didn't come standard in a crumby storage facility like this one flickered overhead. An entire arsenal of weaponry, tactical gear and ammunition stared back at her from organized shelves, tables and cases. In any other circumstance, she might've been impressed, but the fact this container had sat unlocked for weeks charged her with a tendril of panic. Anyone could've gotten inside since Callen was here last. And it was becoming obvious someone potentially connected to Iliana Meyer's disappearance had. "Can you tell if anything is missing?"

"I keep inventory." Callen ducked into the container, heading straight for a bin along the back wall. "Last I checked, I had four Tasers. All the same make and model, but there's only three here."

"Someone was in here." They'd left that Taser at the scene for a reason. Why? Investigators had already combed through the riverbank, dredged the river itself and cataloged all evidence in and around Iliana's abandoned vehicle. What was the point in trying to draw Callen into the case now? Or had it been dropped or discarded during

Iliana's disappearance and police had somehow missed it? "Anything else?"

"It'll take me a couple hours to go through it all." Hours they didn't have. Callen sucked in a deep breath, looking every ounce the private security operator she'd known. On alert, anxious, defensive.

She stepped deeper into the container, noting a collection of hand grenades off to one side and a bulletproof vest on the other. A red light caught her attention from the corner of her eye, and she turned to stare straight up at the small mounted camera in the corner over her right shoulder. Just inside the door. "Does your surveillance system start recording when the door opens or is it designed to run twenty-four seven?"

"When the door opens." His voice dropped an octave, a sure sign of the anger—probably lined with embarrassment at having his space compromised—radiating from within. The tendons and muscles in his forearms flexed under the strain of his fists. "The system pushes a notification to my phone. I know every time that door is opened."

"But I take it you haven't gotten any notifications in a while." So the surveillance probably wouldn't help them. Still, this unit was their best lead. If they could figure out who'd taken Callen's Taser and left it behind at that scene, they could potentially connect them to Iliana's—maybe Lauren's—disappearance. Maeve shut down the urge to run her fingers over the assault rifles—six of them—that hung on the wall from a self-installed grate and pegs. "Who knows about this unit?"

"No one." He finally turned to her then, suddenly so much bigger in this limited space than she'd given him credit for. He'd always been muscular. With his kind of work, he'd had to put in a lot of time building strength and endurance. But now she wasn't sure she could wrap her arms around his middle. Not that she would want to. Unless he asked, which, based on his apology and determination to ensure her he wouldn't come within a foot of her again, wouldn't be in this lifetime. "My parents didn't want me leaving any of this at their house, so I brought it down with me in a trailer. Got the unit under one of my aliases I used in my security work, and I pay for it out of an account in that name. There's no way someone could connect this back to me."

"But they did." She surveyed the rest of the unit in a few seconds. Nothing looked out of place as far as she could tell, but what did she know? "How else could it have shown up at the river?"

"I have a hard time believing police missed it during their search of the area after your forensic analyst went missing." Pulling up something on his phone, Callen swiped his thumb through what she assumed to be his surveillance app. "Which means someone most likely went there to frame me."

"That doesn't make sense. Yes, you have a connection to that place, but not to this most recent victim. If that's what Iliana is." The truth was Maeve had no idea if Iliana Meyer was taken under the same circumstances as Lauren Russell. She couldn't deny the similarities. Both were single women, working in some kind of city or state capacity. Lauren as an urban planner in Springdale and Iliana as a forensic analyst for the State of Nevada. They were close in age, ambitious and came with their own list of enemies. But the biggest resemblance? The fact their vehicles had been left on the bank of the Virgin River nearly one year apart. "Who would want to frame you for Iliana's disappearance? You didn't know her, right?"

"If she was in Zion, there's a chance we came across each other on the trail or in the visitor's center, but no. I've never formally met her, as far as I know." His mouth thinned into a strict line that told her this was getting to him far more than he let on. "Forensic analysts aren't common around here. Considering the increase in homicides, I wouldn't put it past the law enforcement division or Springdale PD to bring one in, but Simpson would've mentioned if Iliana Meyer was in Zion on a case, and I wouldn't have any reason to meet her. Which means she was most likely here on personal time."

She hadn't thought of that. The second she'd heard a vehicle had been abandoned along the same river as Lauren's, she'd gotten in her car and started driving over the state border. No questions. No hesitation. The similarities between the cases had been too great. There was another connection they hadn't talked about, but it hurt too much to think about. Maeve sucked in a sharp breath. "Except Iliana's boyfriend said she didn't have any vacations planned and couldn't explain why she'd come to Zion of all places. As far as I've been able to tell, she doesn't have family or friends here, and she's never been officially called into help with a police investigation."

"I imagine he would say that, considering seventy percent of missing persons cases lead back to the significant other."

Maeve silently counted the number of tear gas grenades organized on the table in front of her. "I have fingerprint dust and brushes in my bag. We can pull prints.

See who's been in here. I can ask the medical examiner to upload the results to the federal database again."

"If they got past my padlock and surveillance system, I doubt they were stupid enough to leave behind prints." He looked at her then, his eyes dipping to her chin then back up to meet hers. "Why the medical examiner?"

Her stomach dropped. "What?"

"You took the Taser to the medical examiner to print and check against the federal database." Turning to face her, Callen blocked off the only exit from the storage unit. Whether he'd done it on purpose or not, Maeve's entire body vibrated with awareness. "Why would you drive thirty minutes out of your way rather than take it to the Springdale PD for processing?"

The ME had asked her the same question, but coming from Callen… She tried swallowing around the dryness in her throat. "Springdale is up against a two-week backlog. They only have one officer available to process evidence at the moment, and they're overwhelmed. The medical examiner's office was the next best option if I wanted results quickly."

It wasn't a lie. Local police often found themselves weeks, if not months, out from processing anything from toxicology samples to processing prints, drugs taken into custody and more. And departments like Springdale, like Zion's law enforcement unit, were always understaffed. But that hadn't been why she had yet to bring the police into her investigation.

A low hum issued from his throat, those intense dark eyes glued to her as though Callen was trying to see straight through her. Her insides clenched because he could. He knew her better than anyone, knew how to get under her armor as though it'd never existed. Knew how far she would go to find the truth and to give the Russells something to hope for. "You haven't just been working Lauren's case the past couple weeks, have you? You've been looking for leads ever since you were removed from the investigation last year."

He couldn't know that. She hadn't told anyone about the suspension, but Callen had always been able to see right through her. Heat flared through her despite the frigid temperatures outside, but there was no point in lying. Callen had his own connections in the law enforcement community. It wouldn't be hard for him to reach out to them and put the truth together, especially since she'd utilized some of his network to run her own investigation without her office knowing. It all connected back to that damn notebook. The one Lauren left behind in her vehicle the day she'd disappeared. Maeve had followed protocol to the letter. She'd documented the notebook's location in the car, its appearance and condition, and confirmed it was Lauren's handwriting inside before sealing it into the evidence bag. But she'd made a mistake in bringing the evidence back to her hotel room instead of filing it with the Springdale PD clerk in the early morning hours when she could barely keep her eyes open. One that would alter the entire course of her career and her life. By the next morning, the notebook had gone missing, and she'd been removed from the case.

"I shouldn't have even been on the case, but I was watching you break a little more each day. You stopped eating. You stopped sleeping. I couldn't get through to you. I was losing you, and it scared me, Callen." Her voice didn't sound like her own. Distant and scratchy. Maeve licked her lips to buy herself time, but he was right about one thing. He deserved to know. "Agents aren't permitted to work cases they might have a personal connection to. It's a conflict of interest, and biases can creep up on you, but she was my best friend. She was your sister, and I couldn't stand there and watch you destroy yourself trying to find her. So I convinced the special agent in charge in the Salt Lake office to let me drive down to assist local PD."

It all felt like another lifetime, her life separating into two different phases. Before Lauren and After Lauren. "Nobody here knew my connection to Lauren, but once that notebook went missing, everything came out into the open. The special agent in charge immediately removed me from the case, and I was suspended. Within a week, the crime scene was released. A month later, the search teams and K9 units were called off. Nobody was looking for her, and I… I couldn't leave her out here. By that time, we'd already split, and I transferred to the Las Vegas office. I had the resources, the anonymity and the proximity to keep searching. There wasn't much to go on though. Until now."

There was a softening in Callen's shoulders. Not a significant amount to convince her he could forgive her for compromising his sister's investigation but enough to tell her he understood what drove her to lie. "The container is making it impossible to access my surveillance feeds. I need to step out." Lowering his phone to his side, he half turned toward the door. "Thank you. For not giving up on her."

Maeve thought she might have nodded as he stepped free of the container. Turning her back to the door, she swiped at her face. She had to pull herself together. Emotion couldn't take the lead in the case this time. Lauren and Iliana were counting on her, and somewhere in this damn freezing box was a clue as to who might've been involved in their disappearances.

Heavy metal hinges protested from behind. She turned in time to see the door swinging closed and rushed forward to stop it. Too slow. Her hands connected with cold steel as scraping sounded from the other side. "Callen!"

The fluorescent lights flickered. Then went out.

Chapter Thirteen

Callen jerked awake.

A splinter of pain rocketed from the back of his head and shot toward his eyes. His head hit something solid but soft, and another round of lightning surged behind his eyelids. Hell. His senses took their damn time coming around. Shadows spread out in front of him, only interrupted by the faint glow of the truck's familiar dark blue control panel. He was sitting behind the wheel of his truck. The engine was running, headlights casting the rushing river through the windshield alight.

His skull lit up as he hit that tender spot against the headrest again, and Callen craned his gaze out the driver's-side window, into the darkness. "What the hell?"

He knew this river. Knew the stretch of riverbank and the slight curve that would take him along the cliffs. He'd walked it so many times trying to find something—anything—to tell him where Lauren might've gone. Only thing he didn't know was how he'd gotten here. The last thing he remembered…

Maeve.

"Oh, good. You're awake." The voice drew his attention to the passenger seat. To the masked man sitting there as though they'd prearranged this meeting in the middle of the night. At a crime scene. "Thought you might never wake up. There were a couple times you came around, but I must've hit you harder than I expected. My bad."

Callen moved to go for the weapon stashed in his center console. Biting pain sang from his wrists, digging in deeper with every pull. He'd been zip-tied to the steering wheel.

"Did you really think I didn't know where you stashed all your weapons?" The passenger leaned forward, popping open the glove compartment. The inside light wasn't enough to highlight much, but Callen clocked the all-black attire as well as the man's build as he extracted one of Callen's tactical knives from within. Powering down the window, his abductor tossed the knife out. The thud registered a split second before the window powered up. The guy was tall. At least as tall as Callen, but not as muscular. The dim lighting and the ski mask placed just right guaranteed he wouldn't be able to pick up on any identifying characteristics. Then again, physical features weren't the only identifiers in Callen's line of work. The way he moved, the way he dressed, even the fluctuations in the man's voice told him this wasn't the first time he'd assaulted someone. "I've been in this truck more times than I can count."

There was no point in asking who the hell this guy was. It was a waste of time considering the mask guaranteed Callen couldn't identify him, but it was obvious he believed he knew Callen. Had access to his vehicle, potentially even his home. Callen fisted both hands, ready to remove the entire steering column if necessary before he beat this guy over the head with it, but an unconscious suspect didn't do him any good. He wanted answers. "What do you want?"

"The same thing I've always wanted, but you, sir, just keep getting in my way." Leaning back in the seat, the man beside him was the definition of relaxed under pressure. How many times had he attacked someone from behind and zip-tied them to the steering wheel? "Well, you're not the only one. Your sister, too. And that other lady. What was her name? Eliza? Isla? Indie? You'd think I'd know after how long I watched her, but they all just start to run together after a while."

Callen's blood went cold. He fisted his hands for an entirely different reason, fighting back the numbness in his fingertips. Lauren. This man had known Lauren. And Iliana. Dread pooled at the base of his spine, but Callen forced his hands to release. "How the hell do you know my sister?"

"Oh, that's not the question you really want to ask, is it, Callen?" His abductor turned dark eyes on him, and Callen had the distinct impression the man was smiling from beneath the mask. "You want to know if I had anything to do with her disappearance. To make it clear, yes. You see, Lauren happened to figure out my little secret, and she threatened to tell on me. I couldn't have that, so I asked her to meet me here. Right at the bank of this river. After that, it was just a matter of making her vanish into thin air. Gotta tell you, though, she was a fighter. More so than Iliana."

Callen couldn't contain the rage, and he threw his upper body across the center console to get to the suspect. "You son of a bitch! Where is she? Where is Lauren?"

"Now, now, Callen. You've got to learn to control that

temper of yours. It's always gotten you into trouble. Ever since you were a kid, right?" His attacker threw his hands up in surrender, though Callen doubted there was a single bone in the guy's body that intended to give in so easily. "Your mommy and daddy got all those calls from the principal about you fighting the other kids. It was any wonder you went into such a violent job in security. Is that why you came all the way down here to be a ranger? Surround yourself with nature and quiet? 'Cause I got to say, it's not working."

Callen's heart threatened to beat straight out of his chest. The words coming out of the bastard's mouth made sense on a logical level, but there was no way the man in the passenger seat could have so much information on him. He sucked in a deep breath through his nose, but there was no calming the raging storm. "Is she alive?"

"Who? Lauren?" The bastard went back to pulling a handgun Callen had hidden beneath the passenger seat. That went out the window, too. Followed by a Taser identical to the one he'd gifted the women in his family all those years ago. No searching. As though he knew exactly where to look. Just pure disarming weapon by weapon. "What do you think?"

A flood of grief hit harder than he expected. He'd known the chances of recovering Lauren alive, but to have her death confirmed by the man seemingly responsible for her disappearance hurt. "I'm going to rip your spine out of your body. Vertebrae by vertebrae until you tell me what you did with her body."

"Now, that's not very nice. Here I am, giving you the information you want, and all you can think about is hurting me. I expected better of a man who claims to want to protect the people he cares about." The slight uptick in the bastard's voice told Callen he was smiling again. "Besides, you already know where she is."

"What do you mean I already know? I've been looking for her for..." Callen froze. No. That hadn't been his sister. He would've known the moment he'd set sights on those remains. Wouldn't he? The mental image of those bones—bleached white—and left for anyone to find refused to budge. What had Maeve said? Caucasian woman in her late twenties or early thirties, who'd never had children or known obesity or malnutrition? "What did you do?"

The words barely strangled free of his throat as his entire body sank deeper into the seat. The dropping sensation sent the blood in his face and upper body fleeing.

"Nothing short of what she deserved, my friend." Familiarity bled into the attacker's voice. Like they'd met before. "So you see, I'm not such a bad guy. I gave you your sister back. Unfortunately for you, your reunion will be short. Because I have a very special agent waiting for me to rescue her from your locked storage unit."

Maeve. The son of bitch had purposefully directed Callen's attention from the woman who'd sacrificed her career to keep investigating Lauren's disappearance. Who'd gotten his parents into therapy and been there for them when he couldn't. All this time he'd thought he was keeping his family together, but it'd been her from the beginning. For no other reason than she cared about them. And she'd taken everything he'd thrown at her—the breakup, the eviction from their apartment, the no contact and cruel words about her character and ability to do her job—without a single word of protest. Without fighting back.

Because he'd convinced her she deserved it. "Don't even think about touching her."

"Why not? You don't want her anymore, do you? That's why you broke up with her and threw her away like she never existed." The masked asshole leaned forward. "Thankfully, I'm here to save her from your ornery ass."

No. Maeve was smart. She would figure out a way out of the shipping container, but he had to buy her time. Keep the guy in the passenger seat talking. "You've been watching us. Watching her."

"Of course I have. That's the best way to learn about a person. You know that from your time working private security." A sigh escaped from underneath the mask as the suspect leaned fully back into the headrest. On any other night, Callen would've thought they were two friends ruminating on the good old days next to their favorite river from the way this guy was acting. Like they were close. Knew each other. "Their habits, their routines. What they like to cook on Wednesdays and which movies they watch over and over. Who they socialize with, who might be a threat to getting what I want. In case it wasn't clear, you're the last one standing in my way."

"You want Maeve." Those three words tasted like ash on his tongue. He didn't have any claim on his ex-fiancée, but Callen sure as hell wouldn't let this son of a bitch get to her. Another part of him couldn't wait to see Maeve protect herself.

"Bingo! Ding, ding, ding! We have a winner." The masked man pointed in Callen's direction.

Buy Maeve time. That was all he had to do. "And Iliana? How does she play into all this? She wasn't a threat to getting to Maeve. She was just a forensic analyst from one of Maeve's first cases. She had nothing to do with this."

"Iliana. That's her name. Can't believe I forgot, but you're right. You're right." Nodding, the stranger dipped his chin close to his chest as though in defeat. It was a ploy, a way to play on Callen's ability to read body language. Take away the threat, catch him off guard, but he wasn't going to fall for that. "Lauren did her job. She got Maeve right where I wanted her, which was away from you, by the way. Her disappearance even worked better than I imagined by leading you to break up with Maeve and toss her out like week old takeout, but I guess I did too good of a job getting rid of her body. Maeve ended up in Vegas, too far for my comfort, you see, so I needed another motivator to bring her back to me."

"So you abducted Iliana Meyer and staged her disappearance to look like Lauren's to draw her in." And he hadn't seen it. Both cases had been connected, but not in the manner he believed. They had nothing to do with him and everything to do with Maeve. "And when Maeve came to Zion you figured she'd come here because of me. So you broke into my storage container, stole one of my Tasers and left it at the scene."

"You really do make things so much more complicated than they need to be, Callen, but I'm not surprised." The man behind the mask laughed, something familiar but out of reach under the circumstances. "Lucky for me, you won't be a problem much longer."

Every muscle in Callen's body tensed. "Why is that?"

"Because you'll be dead." The killer grabbed for the shifter on the steering wheel and wrenched it into Drive.

The truck lurched toward the riverbank as Callen

stomped to hit the brake, but it was no use. The pedal had been removed and the accelerator pinned to the floor. Shoving the door open, his abductor jumped free from the truck cab.

Just as the truck hit the water.

Chapter Fourteen

The shivering wouldn't stop.

That had to be a good thing, right? When she stopped shivering, that was the point she was in trouble? Until then her body was trying to keep her alive. While the unit itself wasn't one of those freezer containers, it seemed Callen had installed an air-conditioning unit to keep his giant plastic bin of C-4 stable in wavering temperatures.

Maeve had shoved against the door with everything she had, but she was quickly losing her strength. She could blame it on exhaustion—mental and physical—from the past few days, but her brain had already filled in the blanks. Her internal organs were slowing function, rerouting energy to her brain and heart. It explained the tingling in her hands and toes. Despite her sweats, socks, boots and jacket, the ache seeped into her joints.

Breathing warmth into her hands, she paced to the back of the container in the short amount of space she found she could navigate without draining her phone battery. She rubbed both hands together to try to generate some kind of heat, but whatever she felt didn't last long. The red light of the surveillance camera hadn't come on when the door closed, and she hadn't heard a single noise from outside the container. Another shiver racked through her. Good. That was good. She still had time.

Though how much, she really didn't know. She'd never been locked in an air-conditioned container before. She couldn't believe how cold it was. The unit had to be close to giving out at this point. Most units couldn't operate below a certain temperature, but it sure as hell felt like it was dropping close to freezing. How long had it been since she was sealed inside? Maeve pulled her phone from her jacket. Thirty minutes. Damn. No wonder it was getting harder to keep her eyes open. Her body wanted to sleep. Only problem was, she probably wouldn't wake up if she gave in. "Think. Think. Think."

Callen's most likely illegal collection of C-4 was guaranteed to blow the door hinges straight off the container, but the blast, in this limited space, would also kill her in an instant. She couldn't use the explosives, and the automatic rifles and tactical gear didn't do her a damn bit of good. There had to be a way. Rushing back toward the door, she gave in to the knot of panic growing tighter and tighter, feeling her way around the frame. Cool metal almost burned her exposed skin as she memorized the area where she thought the padlock might be on the other side.

She was going to kill him for locking her in here. Well, if she didn't die soon. Callen had obviously seen something on his surveillance app that'd given him a clue as to whom might have broken into his personal armory and thought better of bringing her along for the ride. She'd brought him into the investigation—trusted him with details she hadn't shared with anyone else—and this was how he repaid her? Maeve smacked the steel door, pain exploding through her hand. "Callen!"

Damn him. Damn this container. And damn this entire case.

Dragging her phone back out, she checked for a signal, but the walls of the container were too thick. Her battery would last a couple of hours, at least, but at this point she was only holding a brick with a clock. She set her forehead against the door and focused on the next breath. Then the one after that. Her heartbeat pulsed behind her ears, steadying out.

She could do this. She'd been in plenty of difficult situations more life-threatening than this, but given the choice, she'd much rather face one of the serial offenders she'd hunted than a slow, agonizing death or potential murder charges when she got hold of Callen. Shoving away from the door, she willed her vision to fill in the shape of the structure, but the adjustment never came.

"Okay." She just had to slow down. Focus. Callen had built a veritable armory-slash-bunker in this damn container. While they hadn't been in contact over the last year, Maeve knew him better than anyone else in her life. He was security and survival oriented in almost everything he did. Their pantry had been full of canned food, MREs, dehydrated meals and emergency rations. He'd taught her how to process their own chicken broth and make jam, for crying out loud. There was no way he'd moved his entire arsenal without having some survival supplies mixed in. She just had to find them.

And when she got out of this icebox, she would kill him.

She lit up her phone's flashlight feature and scanned the room. Her battery dropped another percent, but it was worth the risk. "If I were an obsessive grump, where would I keep—"

There. Maeve practically lunged for the shelf across the container. The electric lantern flickered to life at the push of a button, lighting up the whole space. Cutting her own flashlight, she almost collapsed back against the table behind her as relief shuddered through her. She could make out Callen's entire inventory without feeling as though the walls were closing in. She pulled the lantern from the shelf, raising it to get a full view of the container. There had to be something—anything—here she could use before turning back to the door. "Would it have been too hard to put a handle or release on the inside of the door? No, no it would not have."

Searching each plastic bin laid out in organized patterns on the tables, she bypassed the explosive—grenades, C-4, what looked like det cord—and moved on to the camping equipment. Nothing that would help her. Her fingers tingled with climbing numbness, making it that much harder to keep her grip on the lantern. Setting it down, she hefted a crowbar off one of the mounted racks and headed for the door. If there was enough room between the door's edge and the side of the container, she might actually have a chance at living. She pressed the thin tip of the crowbar into the corner, but there wasn't any leverage; the two sides of the container met seamlessly. Frustration exploded, and Maeve slid her grip down the bar, using it like a bat. One strike. Two. Each clang resounded through the whole steel structure and shook her straight down to her core, but she and Callen had come in the middle of the night. There was no one here to hear her screams. "What kind of hell is this?"

She dropped the crowbar, out of breath and quickly running out of hope. Out of options. Sinking back against the door, Maeve rubbed both hands down her face. She couldn't remember the last time she'd shivered, though sweat had gathered along her spine from taking her anger out on the door. She set her head back, tapping her skull against the steel.

This was her fault. All of it. If she hadn't lost that notebook during Lauren's missing person investigation, police might've been able to find Callen's sister. If she hadn't taken a case in which she had a personal connection, she might not have been suspended, Iliana Meyer might not have been targeted and she wouldn't feel this monumental dose of failure. All she'd wanted to do was make up for her mistake—for disappointing the people who'd given her everything after she'd lost her dad—but working Lauren's case was only making things worse. She'd given the Russells the hope of finding their daughter, but Maeve didn't see how that was possible anymore. And Callen… He was never going to forgive her for what she'd done. He was never going to be able to see her as the woman he'd loved. Involving him had just been another mistake in a long line of screwups she couldn't shake.

Maeve flexed her fingers, willing some feeling back into them. In vain. Had it gotten colder? The air-conditioning fan seemed to never take a break. She didn't know how that was possible, unless Callen had adjusted it before closing the door. He was out there right now. Going after a potential killer alone. The man was trained to deal with any number of volatile situations, but confronting a suspect wasn't something any agent or officer tackled alone. They'd been partners these past couple of days, and she'd…she'd liked it. Working together, breaking through the hard things with apologies and innocent touches and setting their sights on the same goal. It'd felt like they were a team again. Them against the world.

And she wasn't ready to give up on that.

All right. New plan. Because she hadn't come this far to die here today. Maeve rubbed her hands together again. This time, no amount of warmth came from the friction. She was out of time. She'd gotten a pretty good look at the padlock and its location before stepping into the container. She could guess where it was from the inside, and she happened to have a lifetime's worth of ammunition to test her theory. Pulling one of the handguns free from the mounted rack, she dropped the magazine and collected a box of bullets from the table underneath. In less than a minute, she had a full magazine. She was good with a pistol. Callen had made sure of that.

Sucking in a deep breath, she shoved one of the tables to the other side of the container and took cover behind one perpendicular to the door. There were so many things that could go wrong with what she was about to do, but she no longer had a choice. She would freeze if she didn't get out of here. Gripping the gun between both hands, she leveled the sights around where she thought the padlock might be. Wait. No. She grabbed one of the bulletproof vests and strapped it into place. It wouldn't protect her against a ricochet to the head or neck, but some protection was better than none.

She took aim again. And pulled the trigger. A hole outlined in moonlight appeared where the bullet had gone through the door. Her laugh couldn't be contained. Rushing to the door, she pressed one eye to the hole and gauged where the next shot needed to be. She had to take the risk. Setting the end of the barrel directly against the door and behind the padlock, Maeve took the shot.

The padlock flew off the hinge, and she put her weight against the door. It protested open as a rush of chilled night air—far warmer than inside—swept across her face. She was free.

And without a vehicle.

Callen's truck was gone, but a full set of bars registered on her phone. She tapped his contact information, not sure the number he'd had a year ago would still be in use. "I'm going to kill you and then I'm going to kill you again."

The line rang.

And a cell phone lit up a few feet away. Callen's cell phone.

Ending the call, Maeve collected it from the gravel. The screen had been broken, as though shattered during a struggle. Callen wouldn't have left his cell phone behind. Which meant something had gone wrong when he'd left the container. He hadn't locked her inside.

He'd been ambushed.

Pocketing his phone, she slipped the sidearm into the waistband at the small of her back. "I'm keeping this."

There was only one reason someone may have come after Callen: Framing him for Iliana Meyer's disappearance hadn't worked. His abductor was obviously skilled enough to take down a former security operator, which meant Callen didn't have much time.

It took her brain longer than it should have to work her phone and request a rideshare as it defrosted from near-freezing temperature inside the container.

But she knew exactly where to start the search.

Chapter Fifteen

He was going to die.

Callen pressed his feet into the floor as the river rushed inside the truck. Shocking cold water worked into his boots and up his calves. Faster than he expected. The truck was sinking at an alarming rate, tipping to one side in a losing battle against the current. Any minute now and the entire thing would roll with him inside.

His breathing shallowed to counter the burn of the freezing temperature, but every new inch gained sent his nervous system into overdrive. The hood of the truck disappeared beneath the river's surface, whitecaps cresting against the black metal and illuminated by the headlights. He'd taught every client of his—including his family members and Maeve—how to escape zip ties, but Callen couldn't get the angle right on breaking free from the steering wheel. Every shift, every tug cut deeper into his skin and threatened to sever the nerves and tendons running the length of his hand.

He wasn't going anywhere. Well, that wasn't true. He was going to the bottom of the river. His skull hit the headrest, shooting sparks of pain and lightning across his vision. The water reached his waist, his jeans clinging to him and filling with ice-cold water. The Virgin River wasn't normally this active in winter, but an excess of snow and an unusually hot summer had sloughed enough runoff out of the mountains for this moment.

Callen twisted his torso toward the center console. He'd had a hunting knife stashed in the back pocket of the passenger seat. If the killer hadn't gotten to it, there was a chance he could cut himself free. Except the bastard had claimed to know where every weapon Callen stashed in this truck had been kept. He didn't know how that was possible unless the bastard had somehow gained access to his vehicle, but he couldn't think about that right now. His wrists screamed at the increase in pressure, but he gritted his teeth through it.

Until blood swelled and dribbled into the river water cresting his navel. Damn it. He'd trained for this. How to escape a sinking vehicle. How to use force and momentum to break through zip ties. The combination, however, would be what killed him. Callen kicked at the truck's floor. "Come on!"

Water skimmed along the bottom of the steering wheel, and the truck's headlights flickered. It'd gotten to the electronics, and before he had a chance to prepare himself, the entire truck went dark.

He couldn't see the level of the water, only feel it creeping up his chest. No amount of struggling or shifting his weight would stop it. His skin burned everywhere it touched until he couldn't take a full breath. It was those first few seconds of a cold shower after a workout, jarring and short-circuiting his brain.

He had to calm the hell down. There was a chance he would have more to work with while underwater. Where the lights and the water levels and the fact that he couldn't get his legs free wouldn't distract him. Closing his eyes, Callen sucked in a shallow breath, then another in quick succession. Forcibly hyperventilating expanded his lung capacity. As soon as the water filled the cab or the truck hit the bottom of the river, he could use his feet as leverage to break the ties.

It was the only plan he had. One that would guarantee he'd reach Maeve in time. Because the son of a bitch had locked her in the storage container, and while he had every reason to believe she could take care of herself, the man with the mask had made it clear this plan had been in progress for a long time. There was no way the bastard would just let her walk away.

And Callen wanted that. More than anything, he wanted Maeve to be free of this threat, of this case, of him. She deserved that. She'd spent the past year trying to make up for a single mistake that had altered the course of her life, and all it'd gotten her was heartache. Grief, rejection, loneliness. Despite being there for his parents and doing what Callen couldn't in holding his family together, he was sure Maeve had only accomplished it by sacrificing herself. Because that was the kind of woman she was.

Strong, confident, tenacious. All at the expense of her mental and physical health. She'd risked her career coming to Zion, to work a case that the police had already given up on, and Callen couldn't let it end like this.

He had to get out of here. He had to get to her.

Freezing rapids skimmed his chin, then his bottom lip. He sucked in the deepest breath he could manage as water covered his mouth and nose. Shutting his eyes against the burn, he counted off the seconds, giving his vision a chance to adjust to the shocking cold and limited light from the flickering headlights. Then waited as the last air pocket escaped through the cracks in the door.

The truck was fully submerged. If he had any chance of getting free, it had to be now. Prying his legs free from the limited space between the driver's seat and the pedals, Callen walked his feet up enough to set his boots against the steering wheel—and pulled.

But the steering column refused to budge, and the zip ties remained. Pain lanced through his hands as he shifted for a better angle. He just needed enough leverage to snap the plastic, but his movements were slowing, his joints aching. The cold was getting to him every second he remained submerged, and the pressure in his chest tightened to the point he was already starting to feel the need to inhale.

The truck rocked to the left, the passenger side caving to the river's demands before setting itself right again. Damn it. Callen secured his numb fingers around the steering column and set his feet against the dashboard. Weren't these damn things supposed to detach easily? Or had the killer altered the truck somehow, ensuring he wouldn't be able to escape? Bubbles raced past his lips and out through his nose as he groaned through another attempt. Pressure popped in one ear, filling the canal with freezing water. The effect disoriented him for a few seconds as he blinked to regain his balance.

His lungs screamed for release, every second another lesson in facing his own death. This wasn't how it was supposed to end. He'd known the chances of recovering Lauren after a year were slim. He'd even accepted that poking around the investigation might come back to bite him in the ass, but not like this. Not when he was so close to bringing her home. When Maeve had just come back into his life. Because no matter how much he wanted to deny it, these past two days had shifted something in him. Reminded him of the man he used to be, the one who hadn't hardened himself against feeling anything for anyone other than his parents and brother. The man who'd looked forward to shucking off the tactical gear, locking up his weapons and falling into the woman who caught him every time. He'd gotten a second chance with her coming to Zion. And he'd blown it.

Now it was too late. There weren't enough minutes left to tell Maeve he appreciated what she'd done for his parents. That without her, he might've lost them for good. There wasn't enough time to fix what he'd broken between them and reassure her that she was worth more than the mistake she'd made, even if it'd taken losing her to realize it. She had deserved better, and she needed to know that.

So he wasn't giving up.

Black vines tendriled at the edges of his vision. Gritting through the cutting pain in his wrist, he focused the rest of his draining energy not on prying the steering column free, but on snapping the zip ties. The mechanics made sense. The more force he used, the weaker the binds, but he couldn't get the right angle in such a limited amount of space. His fingers had started aching more than a few minutes ago. From his dropping body temperature or from the lack of oxygen, he didn't know. Maybe both. He didn't have time to think about it or any of the other signs of his body giving out.

The headlights cut off once again. Only this time they didn't light back up. Water had finally short-circuited the truck's electrical system. He was drowning in pitch darkness, with the mere hope he'd manage to determine which way was up when he got out of the damn vehicle. Because he was getting out. He was going to get to Maeve. He was going to stop the man who'd killed his sister, stop him from hurting her.

Trying to break through the zip ties by force wasn't working, and he'd already wasted too much time. He had to come up with another plan. His chest felt as though it would suction in on itself if he didn't get air in the next thirty seconds, but he'd hold out. There was no other option. Bringing his right leg into his chest, he worked his boot free, then stretched his foot into the back seat. The killer had made a show of disarming Callen's weapons right in front of him, but there was no way the bastard had known where he'd hidden every blade. Shoving his foot deep into the passenger seat back pocket, he skimmed his boot along the bottom of the leather.

And hit something solid. A small, serrated flip blade that might've gone unnoticed by most people, even those riding in the back seat. Getting to it with only one foot posed a problem, but if he could—

The current caught the right side of the truck.

He didn't have time to brace for what came next.

In a split second, the whole world flipped upside down. Callen latched on to the steering wheel to keep some semblance of control, but it was no use. Rushing water pressurized in his ears as the truck rolled. Once. Twice.

Pain exploded along the left side of his body as the vehicle caught on what Callen assumed was a log or boulder. His head hit the driver's-side window, and the last of his air reserves escaped. The inky blackness of the river seemed to grow darker, colder as he blinked to keep himself conscious, but it was a battle he was quickly losing.

A rush of water beat against his skin.

Then something warm. Like a hand slipping over his forearm.

Piercing light cut through the darkness, focused on his bleeding wrists still tied to the steering wheel. Biting pain sliced across his skin, but his hand lifted of its own accord. Was this what dying felt like? This weightlessness? Clarity interrupted his drifting thoughts. He hadn't imagined that. Another moment of pain and his opposite hand floated free from the steering wheel.

Long fingers fisted in his T-shirt, pulling him across the truck cab and through the passenger door, and Callen's brain finally caught up. He homed in on the flashlight filling the vehicle and the figure bracing her legs against the truck's frame to get him out. Someone had come for him. Relying on the last few molecules of oxygen in his lungs, Callen fought the current working to entomb him beneath the surface and followed the retreating ray of light upward.

His movement felt slow and uncoordinated—most likely due to the beginning of hypothermia and head trauma—but within a few seconds, he broke through the surface. That first gasp of air burned stronger than he expected, but he would take it over suffocating any day.

Dizziness wavered his vision—just for a moment—as he forced one hand in front of the other to get to the riverbank. Movement registered ahead, his rescuer collapsing down into a section of weeds, out of breath.

Callen dropped to all fours on dry ground, recognition flaring. "Maeve?"

"Miss me?" She dragged herself to her feet.

He had. He put everything into getting upright. "You have no—"

"Well, looky at this happy little reunion." That drawling voice cut through the night. Masked as before, the killer stepped into the pool of light cast from one of the streetlights. "Sorry to be the one to tell you it'll be short-lived."

Maeve's hand went to her waistband. Her empty waistband. Her attention cut over to the pile of belongings she'd made a few feet away. Including a sidearm. "I take it you're the one who locked me in the storage container."

Callen clocked it, taking a single step toward the weapon. This son of a bitch had tried to kill him. The least he could do was return the favor.

"Nah, ah, ah." Unholstering his own pistol, the killer took aim. At Callen. "Now, I've been nice up until this point, but I'm getting real tired of you getting in my way."

The sound of the gunshot ricocheted off the cliffs lining the river.

But the pain never came.

And Maeve dropped in front of him.

Chapter Sixteen

Well, that hadn't been her best decision.

Maeve pressed her fingers to her midsection as she fell to her knees. Directly below her sternum, blood and murky river water coated the skin as she collapsed. It was warm. Warmer than she thought it might be, but considering she'd just spent the past hour or so freezing to death, that wasn't surprising.

"No!" Callen caught her before she hit the ground. Dragging her into his chest, his front pressed against her back, he stretched his legs out on either side of her. His hands pressed into the wound, and a spike of agony drew a brief scream from her throat. "Hang on. Just hang on. You hear me?"

In seconds, his hands were covered in blood specifically meant to stay inside her body. She was all for sharing bodily fluids, but this seemed excessive. She laughed to herself. Callen would've liked that joke. If she hadn't been dying. Another wave of pain cut her inhale short. "Phone."

She'd dropped her belongings in the dirt before diving in to get to Callen. She hadn't had a plan when the rideshare had dropped her off and driven onto their next pickup. Only an intense need to find him. And she had, his truck's taillights flickering from the black depths of the Virgin River. She'd been ready to jump in then, instinctually knowing Callen had been inside, but the current had caught the underside of the truck and flipped it downriver. Her screams had gone unheard as she raced after it. It was luck that a lodged tree had kept the truck from being swept away, giving her the slim opportunity to pull him out.

"You're going to be okay." Sliding out from underneath her, Callen extracted himself before lunging for her pile of stuff. She bit back the pain as he reached for her phone. Bloodied hands swiped across the screen, and the device lit up the terror etched on his face. In seconds, he was right there by her side and had dragged her back into the protective cradle of his thighs. It was so…nice. Just like the night he'd crawled into bed behind her to help her through her nightmare. She supposed this was just a different kind of nightmare. "I'm at the bank of the Virgin River near River Park. I have a gunshot victim. Caucasian female, thirty-four years old. Single entry wound with a 9mm." Pressure skirted along her spine. "No exit wound."

"That's not good." Maeve gasped for her next breath. The bullet was still inside, tearing through her soft organs with every shift. Causing all kinds of damage she couldn't see or feel. No wonder it hurt so much. Nausea caught her in its grip. From the hole in her stomach or from the general blood loss, she didn't really give a damn. Because with nausea came tears, and she was pretty sure Alka-Seltzer wasn't going to help. Her fingers were numb again. Then her toes.

Callen dropped the phone into the dirt. "They're coming, Maeve. Just hang on. Open your eyes for me."

When had she closed them? It took far more energy than she wanted to expend to pry her eyelids open.

"There you are. Stay with me." Callused knuckles skimmed across her forehead, drawing her hair out of her face. The concern rippling off him heated through her drenched clothing.

Dang it, he was handsome. She wasn't far gone enough not to take notice, but she felt the loosening slide of her thoughts. Instead of sticking where they were supposed to for long enough to give each one consideration, they seemed to filter in, then out. And she was just tired. She imagined that had something to do with blood loss, too. She should probably be more worried about the bullet in her gut, but the gentleness in which he was handling her triggered a need to hope she didn't want to feed. "You need to go."

His brows drew together as he studied her face from above. His dark hair had always curled at the nape of his neck when it was wet like this, and she was suddenly aware of how close she'd come to losing him. Again. "What are you talking about? I'm not going anywhere."

"The shooter… He's getting away." She hadn't caught any distinguishing features through the black mask he'd worn, but he was clearly skilled enough to shoot a moving target and held a grudge against Callen. If she was right, the shooter had been the one to ambush them at the storage facility and zip-tie Callen's wrists to the steering wheel before driving the truck into the river. And the chances that the man who'd shot her was tied to the disappearances of Iliana Meyer and Lauren? Very high. See? She was fine. Her brain was still putting pieces together. Maeve tried to shrug his hand off her shoulder.

"The ambulance is on its way. The…police will be here soon. Go. He can't have gotten far."

Ugh. Why was it so hard to talk? Her heart rate ticked up a notch, and the pool of blood beneath her hand expanded. Too bad. She'd really liked this shirt, and it was one of the few she'd packed. A drugging sleepiness stretched through her, making her body heavier. She sank against his chest, counting off the beat of his heart. Strong, steady, grounding.

"Don't you dare close those eyes, Maeve." An intensity she'd never heard before graveled Callen's voice as he shook her awake. "I already lost you once. I'm not giving up on you again, and I'm sure as hell not going anywhere. So you're going to stay awake, and you're going to tell me what the hell you were thinking taking that bullet for me."

She caught her head tipping forward, like those times she'd fallen asleep during a federal briefing she had no business sitting in on or when she hadn't gotten enough sleep the night before a boring lecture in college. "I saved you from the river. Couldn't…have my efforts wasted."

"You sure it had nothing to do with my good looks?" His laugh rumbled through her and shook something loose as he drew his knees up, until all she could see and feel and smell was Callen. She'd missed that sound, missed the way he'd always been quick to smile when she walked through the door at the end of a long, sometimes bloody workday when they lived together. No matter how hard his day had been or how high the tension between him and his brother had escalated, Callen had always been the one to draw her into his arms and hold her until the bad didn't seem so bad anymore. She saw a little bit of the man she'd known now as he tried to keep her in one piece. "He killed Lauren. They were… They were her remains we found at Kolob Arch."

"I'm…sorry." And she was. More than he would ever know. Not just for his loss, but also because Maeve hadn't been able to follow through on her promise to bring Lauren home. To make this right. She'd given the Russells hope, given them every reason to believe this was fixable—that her mistake in losing that notebook didn't actually hinge on their daughter's return—and she'd failed. That drugging darkness pulled harder and harder. Her hand slipped down Callen's chest of its own accord as her entire body went lax.

"Maeve." His voice hitched. She had some sense of his hand pressed against her face, but she couldn't be sure. There were too many competing sensations in her body she couldn't put into words. "Maeve, open your eyes, damn it."

She wanted to. She really did, but her body had stopped listening to her brain's commands. And honestly, it felt so good to just…stop. To be. To sleep. She'd been fighting for so long—her grief over losing her best friend, the self-imposed shame for losing key evidence in the investigation, the derailment of her career and facing the disappointment of the only family she had left, her anger over losing Callen and an entire future she'd never dreamed of having after losing her dad so violently—but right now, none of that seemed to matter.

She was free. She didn't have to keep fighting or try to live up to the promises she'd made herself. She didn't have to keep burning through her inheritance or face grieving families on the worst days of their lives. She didn't have to wonder where she would be if she hadn't lost Lauren's notebook or dream about what her wedding would've looked like had she and Callen stayed together. She could finally just…drift.

"No, no, no, no. Don't do this to me." Something gripped her chin. His hand? It was hard to tell with her senses dulling second by second. "Open your eyes. You're not leaving me again."

Again? Well, now she knew she was dying. Because she hadn't been the one to leave. He'd shoved her out of his life without a moment's hesitation, but the truth was, she'd let him. She'd left her engagement ring on his nightstand, moved her stuff out while he'd been at work and disappeared as effectively as his sister had to save him an ounce more of anguish. She'd taken the easy way out when she should've fought. And wasn't that what hurt the most? Not his rejection, not even the fact that Callen had questioned her abilities as an agent and a future wife, but that she'd let him cut her loose?

She should've clawed and screamed and protested. She should've refused to give up and done something—anything—to stay. She'd found a new family, one that didn't replace the one she'd lost but that cared about her, and she'd thrown it all away out of shame and guilt. Two emotions that'd been running her life for far too long, and she wished she'd been stronger than that. That she and Callen hadn't been drawn back into each other's lives under the current circumstances, that it hadn't taken another woman going missing for them to simply talk after an entire year of gritting through the pain. She wished she'd been honest with him about working Lauren's investigation and reached out to him before showing up at that scene. And she wished things between them weren't so volatile. Because even though she'd somehow survived without Helen and Tommy Russell, and hell, even Cieron, in her life, she'd found a home in Callen. She'd found safety and reliance and assurance that everything would be okay. That she had someone on her side, for once, fighting for her. He'd given her that, and she'd let it slip out of her fingers.

Warmth shuddered up and down her arms like someone was trying to start a fire. It took her a few seconds too long to realize it was Callen forcing heat into her limbs, but that wasn't the problem. She was bleeding out, and there was a damn good chance the EMTs wouldn't reach her in time to stop it.

"S'okay." Maeve wasn't sure if she was forgiving him for all the harsh words, the unanswered messages and phone calls and the breakup, or if she meant right now. Hell, she wasn't even sure if she'd actually spoke. Things were too jumbled up in her head. She just didn't want him to hurt anymore. It was why she'd put herself between him and the gunman. Callen had suffered enough—from her choices—and she couldn't take responsibility for another reason why he'd disconnected from the world.

A blip of a high-pitched siren pierced through the haze thickening in her skull. At least, she thought that was the source of the ringing in her ears. What did she know? She couldn't even feel her body anymore.

"They're here, Maeve. Just hold on a little longer." Callen was still here, still trying to hold her together, but his voice sounded too far away. "Please."

It was the *please* that broke her heart.

Because it was too late.

Chapter Seventeen

She'd died in his arms.

The thirty seconds in which he hadn't felt her pulse as the EMTs raced to intervene had been the longest of his life. Blood and water had soaked through his clothing, but the thousands of glimpses of their life together that'd crossed his brain in that half a minute shattered him.

Callen was still trying to put himself back together as he tracked her breathing from the chair beside her hospital bed. Maeve had woken a couple of times when the painkiller had worn off, then dropped back into unconsciousness. He wasn't sure she even knew he was here, but he wasn't leaving. No matter how many times police and nurses and his mother tried to drag him away. He wasn't leaving her.

The low pulse of her heart rate tracked across the monitor by the bed, nearly putting him to sleep. The bullet had ripped apart the right side of her stomach but thankfully missed her lung, esophagus and any other internal organ, including taking pieces out of her ribs. In reality, the injury could've been so much worse, but he didn't like her being here either. The stubborn, vibrant, challenging woman who'd thrown herself in front of a bullet to save him wasn't here. She was buried beneath drips of painkiller, unconsciousness and bruises he'd memorized in the days since she'd been brought in, like the ones down the sides of her hands he imagined came from throwing herself against his storage container door. Thirteen hours of surgery and a slow rotation of physicians had finally removed every piece of shrapnel, but the recovery would be long and hard. But, knowing Maeve, she'd hate her new diet more.

He intended to be there every second. He owed her that much.

"Any change today?" Helen Russell handed off a cheap cup of coffee that smelled of burning. It was the same hospital-made garbage she'd been trying to tempt him with day after day since he'd called her from the emergency room, sloughing off the ER nurses' attempts to evaluate him for hypothermia and Springdale PD's need for answers. His parents—hell, even Cieron—had arrived within four hours from Salt Lake to help. Though he wasn't sure there was anything any of them could do.

"No." He took the coffee as she pulled one of the other chairs closer to the bed. If he was being honest with himself, it'd become more palatable over the last few times. The offer wasn't much, but it was something for him to focus on instead of all the times he'd failed the woman in front of him. Not just in the past couple of days, but since Lauren had dragged Maeve into his life. Callen forced himself to swallow a mouthful of the tar disguised as coffee. The liquid almost scalded the top of his mouth, but he'd found the more taste buds he killed, the more likely he was to actually finish it and all the crap his parents shoved at him from the cafeteria. "Just you today?"

"Your dad and your brother thought it might be a little

overwhelming if she woke up to find the entire family staring at her." His mom took a drink of her own coffee, wincing at the taste or the temperature, he didn't know. Either way, she cupped the thin, flimsy plastic-coated cup in both hands in her lap. "For that to happen, though, she'd have to wake up, wouldn't she?"

Pain lanced through his chest. He hadn't given himself a lot of time to think of anything more than the shooter who'd pulled the trigger—a shooter who'd evaded a police search of the area—and tracking which nurses and physicians came into the room, but when he did, all he could think about was the fact she hadn't woken up. Not really. "Yeah."

"Did you sleep at all?" Helen sat back in her chair.

He bought himself a few seconds with another mouthful of black garbage. "What do you think?"

Helen sucked in a sharp breath through her nose, a sign she was already preparing herself for today's uncomfortable talk. Just as he had the day before and the day before that. "There's a pullout couch over there. I can sit with her if you—"

"No." He shook his head

"Callen, honey." Her hand slipped over his forearm braced against the chair he'd slept in, ate in and waited in. He knew that tone, and he didn't want to hear it. Not from her. Because she would be right, and he would be forced to see her logic. "You can't take care of her if you're not taking care of yourself, and she's going to need you now more than ever to get through this."

He knew that. "I want to be here when she wakes up."

"You'll still be here. You'll just be lying down over there." His mother pointed to the other side of the private room, where a long bench seat took up position beneath the window. "Don't make me get a nurse to sedate you."

Callen couldn't summon the energy to laugh. She'd do exactly as she threatened if she thought it would help. The problem was the knot tightening in his chest at the thought of putting any more distance between him and Maeve. Which was ridiculous. Because for the past year, he'd ensured there were at least a couple hundred miles between them at all times, but that'd been before she'd pulled him out of that truck. Before she'd stepped in front of a bullet for him. Before he'd learned his sister wasn't ever coming home. "It should've been me."

"You're going to feel that way for the rest of your life." His mother's hand shook as she swiped at her face, and suddenly the years piled into her face, exaggerating the frailness he hadn't noted before, the hollowness in her cheeks. In the blink of an eye, he was looking at the woman who'd lost a daughter a year ago, that same grave pallor leeching color from her face. "And I'm sorry for that, but we both know Maeve will do whatever it takes to prove she's good enough for this family, even if it means sacrificing herself. There wouldn't have been anything you could've done to stop her."

Cutting his attention to Helen, he wanted to lash out, to scream, to hit something. Hard. Callen settled for an inhuman growl and turned back to his ex-fiancée. "She's always been good enough. Throwing herself in front of a bullet doesn't change that."

"Do you really believe that?" Dark eyes—the same color as his—settled on him. Not with hardness or blame, but an exhaustion he felt deep in his bones. "Because I seem to recall you cutting her out of your life as though she never existed. I recall the words you used to describe her after she told you what had happened to that evidence, and I remember you ignoring her calls and messages until you finally blocked and deleted her number. At what point after Lauren disappeared would she have believed she was good enough to be part of this family?"

Shame and a heavy dose of self-hatred burned through him as effectively as the coffee he'd forgotten about. Callen white-knuckled the arms of the chair, not really feeling the pain in his bandaged wrists anymore. The wound in the side of his head from where he'd hit the driver's-side window was another story. "She admitted to compromising Lauren's case. I was angry. I…overreacted."

He knew that now. Hell, he'd known it the moment he'd come home to the apartment to find her stuff gone, but he'd…he'd been too prideful to apologize, to ask her to stay, to admit he needed her. Too devastated facing the knowledge Lauren was gone, that the one thing that could've helped find her had disappeared right along with her.

What he wouldn't give to take it all back. To have Maeve smile at him when he came in a room like she used to, to burrow into her warmth on cold winter nights when no amount of blankets did the job. To feel her wrapped around him in every way and hear the breathless moan she made of his name between the sheets.

"Do you know why your father and I started going to therapy?" Getting to her feet, her purse hanging off her arm, Helen rounded the side of the bed and set her coffee on one of the side tables. She skimmed manicured fingertips across Maeve's forehead, shifting all that long, dark hair out of her face.

"You said Maeve talked you into going because the grief around losing Lauren was too much." Something he hadn't known about until recently. And something he might not ever be able to repay Maeve for. Despite his despicable treatment, she'd stepped in to hold his family together when all he could think about was finding his sister. She'd done the hard work. She'd put his parents first and ensured they made it through to the other side in case her private investigation failed. And maybe that was why he felt the need to stay right here beside her bed as she recovered, but part of him knew the truth. She'd made a mistake in Lauren's investigation, but he'd never stopped caring for her. The past few days had stripped him of the wall he'd built between them brick by brick. Exposing everything he'd tried to deny over the past year. He still loved her. Wanted her.

"Part of that was true." His mother trailed her fingers across Maeve's brow, but there was no response from the woman lying unconscious in the bed. "But, really, we went for her."

That didn't make sense. Callen shook his head. "I don't understand."

"This girl has witnessed unimaginable violence in her life, with no one to help her through it. Her mother left when she was just a toddler, and her dad… Well, we both know she saw more of what happened than she tells us." Shock only had a split second to sink in before Helen Russell raised her knowing gaze to his. "Don't get me wrong. She's learned to cope and compartmentalize because she has to. It's part of her job. She steps into the lives of people who have suffered like she has, in hopes of turning out a different outcome. She faces danger with no thought of herself, but when Lauren disappeared and you ended the engagement, Maeve was broken."

His attention cut to Maeve, but he couldn't reconcile the woman who'd stood up to him on the trail over the skeletal remains of his sister with the woman his mother was describing. Maeve was a federal agent. She came home every night after chasing serial offenders—working her way up through the FBI—with a smile on her face the moment she stepped over the threshold and jokes she'd heard at the office. This was the woman who'd cried in front of him only once, at her father's funeral, and went out of her way to ensure he wasn't stretching himself too thin. The same woman who'd directed Cieron through Narcotics Anonymous and acted as a victim advocate on her days off. Not once had she given him the impression she was capable of anything close to the word *broken*. That wasn't the agent who'd stood up to him these past few days, and it sure as hell wasn't the woman he'd planned on spending the rest of his life beside. But his mom had never been a liar, and she had no reason to start now.

Callen leaned forward in his chair, stiff and exhausted and angry and exhausted some more. "What are you saying, Mom? That Maeve asked you and Dad to come with her to therapy?"

"No, dear. We were the ones to force her to go." Defeat weighed heavily on his mother's shoulders, and her purse shifted down her arm. "After she goaded a suspect she had in custody into stabbing her."

Chapter Eighteen

"You look like crap."

That grumble didn't belong in the too-white room with the burning fluorescent lighting. Actually, she couldn't remember the last time she'd heard it and really couldn't figure out what it was doing here. Maeve's stomach felt as though it was eating itself. Or maybe it was the "You're not the brother I was expecting."

"You wound me." Cieron Russell looked nothing like Callen, with his pitch-black hair and high widow's peak. It stuck up in all kinds of directions like he'd run his hands through it. And that, she could relate to Callen. Maybe some habits were genetic. The tight white polo-shirt he wore accentuated a thinness only achievable through copious amounts of drugs. The sickly color of his skin, too, but he looked…better than the last time she'd seen him. Healthier. Thick eyebrows matching the color of his hair hiked higher up a broad forehead and accentuated the five-o'clock shadow her near-brother-in-law had let grow in. Cieron placed both hands over his heart and leaned back in his chair as though he'd been shot. "Here I was doing my brotherly duty in watching over you, and all I get is lip."

Ugh. Now that she'd thought it, she couldn't ignore

the pinch of pain in her gut. Bad choice of…thoughts. Maeve tried to sit up but didn't make it far, closing her eyes against the rush of nausea surging up her throat. "You started it."

Was she slurring her words, or was that her imagination? She wiggled her toes and fingers. She couldn't feel them, but they were there under the sheets, and they were responding. That was a good sign, right? No paralysis. The bullet must've missed her spinal column.

Callen's voice echoed through her head. He'd said that right after…after she'd taken that bullet the shooter meant for him. The machine monitoring her heart rate ticked up in tempo. The pressure in her chest expanded. While the bullet might've missed her spinal column, it felt like her insides had been shredded. Probably not inaccurate. "How long have I been out?"

"Almost four days." Crossing one ankle over the opposite knee, Cieron watched her with that unnatural stillness he sometimes took on. An intensity she'd never been able to achieve, even in the middle of an interrogation. She'd always envied him for that.

Then she registered what he'd said. "Four days—"

"You woke up a couple times, but from what I hear from Mom and Dad, this is the most lucid you've been." He interlaced his fingers across his stomach, and another wave of discomfort fired through her.

"Your parents are here?" She quit trying to sit straight up and simply tried to keep herself from throwing up all over the bed.

"Callen called them." That all-too-familiar hint of resentment brothers carried for one another—especially two only eleven months apart in age—tainted Cieron's voice. "As you can imagine, he calls, they jump. Like the prodigal son returns, or some shit. They were on the road within a few minutes of getting the news you'd been shot and were admitted to surgery."

Callen. The memories were there, right at the cusp of her mind. Him holding her as she bled out. His refusal to chase down the suspect. The concern in his voice, his demands to keep her eyes open. It all played out in a sickening display. Though now that she thought about it, she'd been wrong to tell him to pursue the shooter. The man had told Callen he was responsible for Lauren's death. The suspect could've easily turned that gun on Callen, and there would've been nothing she could've done about it.

Maeve settled back against the pillows, overwhelmed just by this conversation. Exhaustion increased the heaviness in her eyes as she set her head back. "Where are they?"

Did Cieron realize she wasn't really asking about Helen and Tommy?

"Cafeteria." Cieron motioned toward the door with a jut of his chin. "You know how Dad gets when it comes to hospital food."

She did know, but she didn't want to think about that or why Tommy Russell had been in that hospital at all. The thought of her father-in-law shoving endless hospital cafeteria hamburgers in his mouth nearly made her sick to think about. Maeve opened her eyes. Except Tommy wasn't her father-in-law. He wouldn't ever be.

And that hadn't been the point of her taking on Lauren's case alone—to convince Callen to give them a second chance—but it hurt all the same. Almost more than the gunshot wound to her abdomen. "And Callen called you?"

A flash of too-white teeth—all veneers, considering the last time they'd come face-to-face was when he'd overdosed in an empty warehouse from the crap he'd injected into his arm—gave the slightest impression of his relation to Callen. "Mom threatened to take away my allowance money if I didn't join their merry band of concerned citizens."

She'd underestimated how much energy it took to work around Cieron's sarcastic personality and dig out the truth, and she just didn't have the patience for it now. A weight that had nothing to do with the hole in her stomach pressed into her chest, making it that much harder to inhale.

If the shooter had been telling Callen the truth, Lauren was dead. Her sole purpose for putting one foot in front of the other for the past year was gone. And she didn't know what to do with that right now. But Iliana Meyer was still out there, still missing under the same circumstances as Lauren had been, and while Maeve had already taken a look at the forensic analyst's financials, phone records and GPS, she got the sudden urge to do so again. To do something while forced to remain in this bed. "Well, if it's permission you're looking for, you can leave."

"Unfortunately, I was also threatened with losing my favorite body part if I didn't hold down the fort by my oh-so-loving brother." That smile was back again, the one that told her Cieron had no intention of following through his brother's demands. He never had before. Why start now?

"Callen has always had a way with words." Turning

her head to face Callen's brother, she fought back the burn of emotion battling to take over. Not just from what'd happened at the river or the past few days since coming face-to-face with her ex-fiancé again, but for all the times the bad guys had won. Her mother leaving, her father's murder, the suspect responsible for the scar around her navel, that damn notebook of Lauren's. Her eyes burned. Crap. The pain medication was doing too good of a job of breaking down her defenses. "I'm sorry about your sister."

The humor drained from Cieron's face. She'd never seen him take on such a serious edge. Like he'd become a different person altogether. "That wasn't your fault."

She nodded. At least, she thought she did. "But I promised you I'd bring her home."

It'd been an agreement between them after finding him high out of his mind in that warehouse. She'd never told Callen what'd happened, how his mother had come to her, afraid Cieron was using again. That he might be dead. He hadn't been seen in almost a week, his apartment empty, missed calls from his employer on the cell phone she'd recovered. Four days. It'd taken her four days of pestering his friends and ex-girlfriend for information, contacts, buyers and favorite spots to crash. He'd barely been breathing when she found him shivering underneath a threadbare blanket with mice and raccoons closing in to claim him as soon as his heart stopped. The NARCAN she carried had done its job countering his opioid overdose, and she'd gotten him straight to the emergency room. He'd come around a few days later, promising to go into rehab. If she found his sister.

Cieron scrubbed both hands down his face. No new track marks along the insides of his arms. He was clean as far as she could tell, his eyes clear. "You kept our deal, Maeve. You found her."

The hospital room door opened, putting Callen directly on its threshold. His shoulders broader on a deep breath as he studied her from head to toe and a burn that had nothing to do with the room's temperature following his gaze's path.

"That's my cue." Cieron extracted himself from the chair and headed for the door without so much as stopping to acknowledge his brother. "Don't die, Maeve. You're the only one in this family who doesn't make me want to bang my head against the wall."

Callen waited until the door had closed behind his brother before approaching the bed. "You're awake."

A flood of familiarity washed through her, deep and intoxicating. That voice had kept her sane more times than she wanted to admit, and hearing it now reminded her they'd survived whatever game the shooter had put into play. Maeve settled back against the pillows, her eyes heavier than they'd been a couple minutes ago. "Dying isn't for the weak. Zero out of ten. Don't recommend it."

A smile cracked at one corner of Callen's mouth as he took a seat, but it didn't reach his eyes. The tightness around his mouth told her his concern had gotten the best of him. She wasn't out of the woods yet. With a wound like hers, any number of things could go wrong, and with her luck, they just might. "You hungry?"

"I'm..." She didn't know what she was. Hungry? Tired? Stressed? Relieved? All the above? The pain was still there, ebbing and thrashing in the background with each inhale, but it was manageable. "I don't know."

"The doctor said your appetite might take a couple

of days to recover, and you won't be able to eat as much as you did before." The near-monotone way he recited those words hurt her heart. He was taking this personally, claiming responsibility for her ending up in this hospital.

And she couldn't have that. Callen had suffered enough. First losing Lauren, then taking the sole weight of trying to be everything for everyone in his family. Not to mention almost drowning. "You mean I can't eat an entire pizza by myself in the dark anymore? There go my plans for Friday night."

The laugh that choked out of him filled the room and ticked the pulse on the monitor higher. Real. That one was real. She'd always loved the sound of his laugh, rumbling and smooth and deep. The perfect combination to light up any horrific day. Because as long as Callen could laugh, life couldn't be bad. He took Cieron's seat like he'd come onto a shift. "I'm sure whatever lucky guy you've got waiting for you in Vegas can help with that when you get back."

Back. The case that'd brought her to Zion was over, if the shooter had told Callen the truth. Lauren was dead, her remains currently spread across a stainless steel examination table in the basement of a funeral home, but Iliana Meyer? She was still out there. She could still be alive, and while Maeve was sure Springdale PD was doing its job, she could help. No, she wasn't going back. "There isn't anyone waiting for me. There isn't…anything left for me in Vegas."

Surprise widened Callen's eyes. "I find that hard to believe."

She couldn't contain the humorless laugh charging free from her chest. It tugged on the surgical dressing taped beneath the ugly gown she'd been shoved into and antagonized whatever closures—staples or sutures—below her sternum. "How can I possibly have anyone waiting for me, Callen, when all I've been able to think about over the past year is you?"

Chapter Nineteen

She hadn't meant that.

Callen couldn't move, couldn't breathe. His skin suddenly felt too hot. He fisted both hands against the chair's arms, igniting a flare of pain in his lacerated wrists. If he'd been hooked up to the heart rate monitor currently pounding through his brain, she'd know. She'd know how much her words affected him, how much he wanted them to be true. Because he'd been lying to himself all this time. Since the day he'd found her engagement ring on the nightstand and her belongings moved out, something inside him had become unfixable. Like she'd broken off a piece of his soul and taken it with her to Vegas. His anger toward her—his blame—had distracted him enough for him to focus on the job in front of him and dig deeper into Lauren's investigation, but he'd just been lying to himself. Hadn't the past few days proved it? The cracks in the wall he'd built between him and the rest of the world—especially her—weren't just slivers anymore. They'd grown.

Her staying in touch with his parents.

Her risking her career to privately work Lauren's case.

Her pulling him from the truck.

Her taking the bullet meant for him.

Each crack had fissured into gaping holes now puncturing his defenses, and Maeve was at the center of it all. His ex-fiancée, a woman who should hate him with every fiber of her being, had sacrificed everything to put him and his family first. And he'd cut her out of his life as though she'd meant nothing.

He didn't deserve her. He didn't even deserve to breathe the same air as her. He'd done nothing but try to tear her apart piece by piece since he'd confronted her on that trail, and now she was telling him she hadn't moved on with someone new since they'd broken up? That she still thought about him?

Clearing his throat, Callen leaned forward, setting his elbows on his knees. Every muscle in his body ached from being inside that damn truck when it'd gone into the river, but he'd take the sensation over the numbness he'd allowed himself to slip into since coming to Zion. It was only in the past few days that he'd felt anything. Because of her. "You've been through a lot the past few days—"

"Don't." The sharpness in her voice silenced the part of him that wanted to deny her claim. "Don't do that. Don't twist my words until they fit whatever narrative you've told yourself since we broke up."

His heart nearly jerked to a full stop. "I hurt you."

"Yeah. You did. But it doesn't change the fact I never stopped caring about you." The color had come back into her face over the last four days, but it would take much longer for him to stop seeing the blood bubble out of that gunshot wound, to stop feeling it coat his hands. "How could I not, Callen? You were there after my dad died. You stayed with me at the police station so I didn't have to be alone, and you…you found the man responsible.

Lauren was my best friend, but you? You were the one who put me back together."

Callen didn't know what to say to that, what to think. Everything she'd just said settled like a rock in his stomach. He wanted to deny it all, tell her he was nothing compared to the courage and determination and protectiveness she'd displayed just since she'd come back into his life. "You weren't broken."

"Yes, I was. I just didn't know it until I fell in love with you. You were there when the nightmares got to be too much. You made me feel wanted when you proposed and went out of your way to make sure I felt included in your family, made me feel like I was loved." Her voice wavered, and suddenly Callen couldn't help but feel too far away. That he should be touching her, telling her it was okay. That she didn't owe him anything. "And you supported me when I applied to be a field agent and iced all my bruises and scrapes from training."

His laugh surprised him. "There were a lot."

"I remember." Her answering smile hitched his next breath. She didn't do that often enough, even before Lauren had gone missing, and Callen tucked this one away in his mind so he'd never forget it. "My point is, you gifted me with something far more valuable than an engagement ring or a place to live or nights I didn't have to spend wrapped up in my own head alone. You were my light in a world of darkness. You showed me how to feel safe again. How could I ever expect to find that in someone else?"

Someone else. She hadn't been with anyone since him? A possessiveness he had no business feeling thickened in his veins. His mouth twitched under the release of pressure from his chest. All this time he'd imagined some guy warming her bed, settling her chaotic thoughts with kisses and touches that'd once been his and grounding her through her nightmares. For nothing. And those moments she talked about? They didn't feel like anything big, but according to Maeve, they'd changed her life.

A life that had almost been cut short. Twice.

His smile slipped, his blood growing cold as his mother's admission surged to the front of his mind. "Then why did you provoke a suspect into stabbing you?"

The color she'd regained in her short recovery drained, accentuating the dehydration lines streaking through her lips. It didn't matter how many liters of blood and fluids she'd received, it would take weeks for a full recovery. "How do you…how do you know about that?"

"My mom mentioned the real reason she and my dad started going to that trauma therapist." The tension that seemed to squeeze his insides since his mother had filled him in on exactly how bad things had gotten for Maeve after the breakup only tightened. She'd been hurting—almost died—far more than he'd expected after the breakup, and he hadn't known. "You didn't recommend her to them. They went for you. Because they were worried about you."

"Getting injured in the field is always a risk. That's part of the job—"

"Don't." He used her earlier words against her. "Don't tell me what you think I want to hear to make this conversation go away. It won't work. I know the truth." Callen physically fought down the nausea that came with the burn of acid on his tongue as he forced the words. "Your partner was the one to call my parents to the hospital.

They were still listed as your emergency contacts. He told them everything, including the lie he'd filed in his report to protect you from losing your job. I know you went to that house to arrest a suspect in connection to the serial case you were working. I know he was suspected of killing two other female law enforcement officers, but you took the case anyway. I know you and your partner split up that night to search the house. And I know you didn't draw your weapon when he charged you with a knife."

Her throat worked on a shallow swallow. She couldn't deny it. He'd already reached out to one of his FBI contacts to confirm what his mother had said. He'd read the false report and talked with her former partner in the Salt Lake office. There wasn't anything she could hide from him now.

"You spent three weeks in the hospital, seventy-two hours of that under a suicide watch because my mom thought you might hurt yourself. Why?" That single word scraped up his throat as though he'd been yelling for hours. Softening his voice, Callen shifted to the edge of the bed. To get closer to her, to touch her, to just neutralize the buzz beneath his skin he'd lived with for the past four days while she'd been unconscious. "Why wouldn't you defend yourself, Maeve? I know you know how. I've seen you do it a thousand times, and like you said, you're a damn good agent. You could've stopped him, and you chose to let him hurt you."

Tears glimmered in her eyes. Only once had she ever cried in front of him during her father's funeral. He wasn't sure whether it was because of the emotional onslaught of loss then or because Maeve didn't allow herself to show that kind of vulnerability over the years. And, hell, he'd done nothing in the past year to show her she was safe with him anymore, but he wanted to be good enough for her now. "Why, Maeve?"

"Because I failed." Her shoulders shook on a sob, and Callen only shifted closer, pressing his weight into her side like he'd done during her nightmare the other night in his house. "I screwed up Lauren's case, and you were so angry." She closed her eyes but somehow found the courage to face him again. "You had every right to get as far from me as possible. I knew that, but knowing something like that and facing it… I failed you. I failed your parents, who'd given me everything. I've lost everyone I ever cared about, but Lauren, it was my fault. I realized I wasn't the woman you thought I was, and I couldn't handle the fact I couldn't fix it, and in that moment, that suspect, he just made it so easy."

He couldn't keep his anger in check. Over the time he'd wasted blaming her, over the hateful words he'd spewed at her, over the assumption that she hadn't done enough or that she was anything less than the strong, compassionate woman he'd fallen in love with. Callen pressed his forehead to hers, closing his eyes, taking her in.

"You never failed me, Maeve. You made a mistake, but that mistake doesn't equal your worth. Not to my parents, and sure as hell not to me, and I'm sorry if I ever made you feel like you weren't worth loving. Because I forgive you. You are…you are amazing, and it took me far too long to realize what an idiot I've been when it comes to you." Skimming his thumb beneath her trembling bottom lip, Callen caught a renegade tear as it broke free from her lashes. "I haven't been with anyone either."

Her watery gaze raised to his as he leaned back.

"I tried. I had one of my security friends set me up, but it felt all wrong. I thought maybe it was too soon after the breakup, so I waited a couple months before going on another date, but that one felt wrong too." But this? Her warmth radiating into his hand, her breath skimming across his bruised knuckles, her scent still clinging to his clothes? It settled some feral part of him he'd tried to ignore, tried to forget existed but had run rampant since she'd left. "It took me a while to realize food stopped having any taste. I haven't been able to get to sleep without taking something since I came to Zion. I think about you all the time, and I convinced myself you ruined everything between us by mishandling evidence in Lauren's investigation, that if I hurt you the way I hurt, I would feel some kind of justice. But after being with you the past few days, knowing you've risked everything to be here for my sister, I realize I'm the one at fault. The things I said, I didn't mean them, Maeve, and I'm sorry."

Her hand slipped over his as she leaned into his touch. "Me, too. I'm sorry about Lauren. I shouldn't have dragged you into this case. You almost died—"

"There isn't anything you have to be sorry for. I made the choice to get involved. There wasn't anything you could've done to stop me, and I'm glad we found her. It's not what I'd hoped, but she can come home now. She's not scared or in pain or alone, but Iliana Meyer is still out there, and we need to find her." His phone vibrated from his jeans pocket. Callen unpocketed the device, and dread spiked through him. Leaning back, he turned the screen toward Maeve with the text message displayed. It's Simpson. The rangers have found more remains.

Chapter Twenty

They couldn't keep her here.

Maeve held her internal organs in with the press of her hand as she shuffled toward the end of the bed. Callen had stepped out into the hallway to call the division head of the law enforcement rangers, but all she'd heard through the door was that the remains were on their way to the medical examiner's office. So that was where she was going.

Just as soon as she figured out how to breathe and walk at the same time again. It didn't use to be so hard, did it? The paper-thin gown gaped in the back, and a frigid slip of air skimmed down her spine. No problem. She wasn't walking out of here with her ass hanging out anyway.

Something twisted in her stomach when she took her next breath. Setting one hand on the end of the hospital bed, she tried not to die. And to mentally untwist whatever didn't like her upright. This was stupid. She knew that, and yet she'd made dumber decisions throughout her life, and she was still here. She'd trained as a federal agent, for crying out loud. Walking ten feet to the pile of neatly folded clothing—probably by Helen's hands—shouldn't be such a task. Maeve struggled for her next breath, counting the seconds she had until Callen walked back in the room. "You managed not to shoot yourself in a refrigerated storage container. You can do this."

It took more effort than she expected to get her feet moving and to hold her weight on her own two legs, but she managed to make it to the chair. Helen wouldn't have left a clean stack of clothes for her if she hadn't expected her to use them, right? Or maybe Callen's mother really just knew her that well. Maeve swallowed the ball of emotion lodged in her throat as she shifted the stack of what looked like jeans, a T-shirt and undergarments into one hand and took a seat.

She didn't blame Helen for breaking her promise not to reveal the details of Maeve's hospital stay after she'd been stabbed. It hadn't been Maeve's place to demand that from the mom who'd stepped into her life in the first place, and she'd known keeping something like that—her rock bottom—wouldn't stay between them forever. She just hadn't wanted Callen to think any worse of her, that she would stoop so low as to drag him back into her life by putting herself at risk. Because he would've been there had he known. He would've set aside his hatred for her in an instant and blamed himself, and she didn't want that.

She'd told him the truth earlier. Those seconds in which her hand had flinched to unholster her weapon as the suspect came at her and her choice not to follow-through had nothing to do with him. She could've easily drawn her sidearm. She'd chosen not to. Not only because of that sick sense of failure that had nipped at her heels since Lauren disappeared, but from the knowledge that she'd truly believed she deserved the punishment at the time. Looking back, she could pinpoint the signs of the deterioration of her mental health, and Helen and

Tommy forcing her into therapy—forcing their support—had worked wonders since, but she hadn't seen it then. All she'd been was empty.

That wasn't the case anymore.

She'd lost Lauren—okay, she'd lost more than that—but she felt as though she was finally able to take her first real breath in months. Closing her eyes, she leaned into the warmth Callen's apology had created until it filled the cold place in the center of her chest she spent so much wasted time trying not to think about. It had heated with his hand on her skin, his thumb tracing the line of her bottom lip. In that moment, there'd been nothing—no investigation, no history, no hurt—but the feel of his skin against hers.

But that chilled emptiness was beginning to return.

With every second she didn't tell him the truth.

Maeve made slow work of dragging her jeans up her legs, careful not to bend too much and piss off the sutures in her stomach. She was out of breath by the time she managed to secure the button and needed a minute before attempting to wrangle her bra.

A minute she didn't get.

The hospital room door opened, and Callen froze as his gaze landed on the bed. Her empty bed. It didn't take him long to register her sitting in the chair across the room. "Get back in that bed."

"Too late." She sucked in another breath as she clutched the bra Helen had either found or bought. It took her longer than it should have for her to recognize it as one of hers. In fact, all the clothes were hers, but she hadn't brought them from Vegas. Maybe items she'd left behind in Callen's apartment? A load of laundry she'd forgotten?

Kind of made her wonder why her ex hadn't burned them or mailed them. Or maybe he'd planned to and Helen stopped him. That woman was always thinking ahead and seemed to sense more than she was willing to admit. "I'm already dressed."

The door closed behind him automatically as he crossed the room to meet her. Tearing her bra from her hand, he towered over her with his phone in the other. "Are you out of your mind? You're four days postsurgery from a gunshot wound. You're lucky you haven't torn anything."

"To be honest, I'm not so sure I haven't." Being out of breath wasn't helping anything. This conversation would go over so much easier if she could stand. "But if I have to spend another minute in that bed knowing your ranger friends recovered a second set of remains, I might stab someone."

Because that second set might belong to Iliana Meyer. Could tell them who had locked Maeve in that storage container, put a bullet in her stomach and tried to drown Callen. Could tell them who had killed Lauren and left her bones to erode beneath Kolob Arch. He knew that, and he had to know there was nothing that could stop her from seeing this through to the end. Even with a GSW in her gut.

He tightened his fist around her bra, and Maeve couldn't help but squeeze her thighs together at the sight of all that muscle in his forearm flexing around black lace, which only hurt more. Nothing in their earlier conversation had hinted at Callen's thoughts on how they moved on after the investigation—together or apart—but it was easy to imagine picking up where they'd left off. Had he thought about it? Was that something he wanted? He'd forgiven her—words she'd ached to hear since the moment she moved out of their shared apartment—but did that mean more to her than it meant to him? "You're not going to let this go, are you?"

"Bingo." Reaching for her bra, she moved to pull one arm through the gown's sleeve but ran out of energy. Maeve set her head back against the wall. She was going to make it all the way to Hurricane and the medical examiner's office. She just didn't know how yet. "Could you please help me? I'm stuck."

"You're going to be the death of me, aren't you?" Callen didn't give her a chance to answer as he tucked his phone in his back pocket and grabbed the hem of her gown. He made quick work of the ill-fitting fabric, exposing her upper body in one fell swoop. "Holy hell, Maeve. How did you get to the chair?"

"It's not that bad." She couldn't fight the urge to look down, her skin puckering against the chill coming through the air-conditioning vents. There wasn't a self-conscious bone in her body. She took care of herself for the most part, and there wasn't a lick of skin Callen hadn't seen or worshipped while they were together. But she could admit this was different. A piece of gauze and medical tape covered the surgical opening, but rounded bruises—black, green, some purple and blue—haloed the surrounding tissue. She sucked in a shallow breath, not daring to move a single muscle. "Okay. It is that bad, but I'm still not getting back in that bed. Help me up."

They worked as a team, going slower than she wanted to go, getting her into her bra, then her shirt. Callen knelt in front of her as he tied the laces on her boots, her hands on his shoulders for balance. He was warm and strong and devoted to the point of putting his life on the line, and she couldn't help but revel in a little bit of that now. While she still had him here. "Any sign of the shooter?"

"Hard to find a man who likes to dress up in ski masks." He switched to her opposite foot. "Springdale PD has the bullet you were shot with. They're running ballistics to see if there's a match in the federal database, but it's going to take some time. You had the right idea cutting the line by going to the medical examiner's office for those prints."

"A lot of good it did us. We still have no idea who broke into your storage container and took one of your Tasers to place at the scene." Or a motive that told them why. Why Lauren? Why Iliana? Why try to kill Callen? Three people in her personal and professional life, all tied through violence. It didn't make sense. If this had something to do with one of her past cases, why not target her directly? Why go through the people she cared about? When would it stop? Maeve swallowed, not liking that line of thinking at all or the fact that Helen and Tommy Russell might be pulled in front of the next bullet.

Callen's hand slid up the back of her thigh as he finished tightening her laces, his body heat penetrating through her jeans. It was almost enough to make her believe they could work things out when this case was done. Almost. "We'll figure it out. Together."

Together. Her eyes burned again. Damn painkillers.

Rising, Callen threaded his arm behind her lower back and dragged her into his side. "Put your weight on me. I can handle it."

The meaning of that sentence went unsaid. *I can han-*

dle you. But she couldn't feed into that hope right now. No matter how much she wanted to. The shooter was still out there. Iliana was still out there, and Maeve needed to find her. Before Callen learned the truth. She settled into his side as they shuffled toward the door in some kind of weird three-legged race. "You couldn't take it that one time we almost fell down the stairs."

"That was different. You jumped out from behind the bedroom door and tackled me." His hand tightened around her back as he tugged open the door. "I wasn't prepared to be attacked after three days on the road, let alone in my own apartment."

Her smile came naturally at recalling the look of utter surprise on his face. Right before they hit the ground in a fit of laughter and kisses and touching that turned wildly inappropriate. It'd been one of the core memories of their relationship, mere days after he'd asked her to marry him. The happiest she'd ever been. Maeve slid her hand over his chest. For balance and nothing more. At least, that was what she told herself. Because moments like that didn't last. They were always overtaken by the bad. "A security operative should always be prepared for an attack."

"Can't argue with you there." He gazed down at her as they navigated their way to the elevator, and the hospital—the PA systems, the rush of nurses and wheelchairs, and too-bright lighting—faded away. There was only him. The only man she'd ever wanted. And couldn't keep. Callen lowered his mouth to her ear, whispering, and a shiver chased across her shoulders. "I still plan to make you pay for that little stunt."

Chapter Twenty-One

"It's not her." Maeve's voice almost gutted him, but it was her struggle to stay standing beside the examination table that had Callen moving. She grabbed backward for the nearest chair, barely catching herself as he settled her in her seat. She'd lost more color from her face and neck. Whether from the realization they were no closer to finding her missing forensic analyst or from her wound, he didn't know. "It's not Iliana Meyer."

"Ms. Perry is right. These remains belong to a male victim." The ME, Dr. Yarrow, his name tag said, came around the end of the stainless steel table. Callen had never been in a morgue, but the forensic pathologist had taken a cold, uninviting refrigerated room and turned it into something worthy of the families who came to identify their loved ones. The older man cast a glance toward Maeve, then cut his gaze back to the second ranger in the room.

"I had patrols spiral out from where the first set of remains were left over the past few days." Ranger Murray Simpson folded his arms across his broad chest, unnecessarily exaggerating his size. The former Salt Lake police officer was easily a foot taller and a foot broader than Callen and Dr. Yarrow, stretching his Zion National

Park uniform almost to its breaking point. "These were recovered a few hundred meters from Kolob Arch about four hours ago. As you can see, they're more worn, been exposed to the elements for far longer and broken in some places compared to the ones you found. We brought back as many pieces as we could find, but animals and weather did a number on what was left."

"They don't smell like bleach, and they're definitely not as white as..." Callen swallowed back the dryness in this throat. "As Lauren's remains." He didn't know whether that was a good thing or a bad thing. Whether so many differences between the two sets of remains told them anything, or they'd come across something entirely unconnected to his sister's investigation. He also didn't know whether Lauren was being kept in this exact room or she'd been moved somewhere else, considering they now had an ID. He squeezed Maeve's shoulder, feeling her pulse ratchet higher under his hand. For the longest time, he'd assumed she didn't allow herself to feel anything—the abandonment of her mother, the loss of her father, her feelings toward him after the breakup—but the utter devastation etched into her expression told him she felt it all. That she felt too much. "Do you have an ID?"

"I took dental scans as soon as rangers brought him in. I'm just waiting for confirmation. He's male, so it can't be your missing victim as Ms. Perry noted." Dr. Yarrow made another pass along the examination table, once again studying Maeve from where he stood, and Callen's hackles rose. That was the second time the medical examiner had referred to her as *Ms.* instead of *Agent.* The doctor slid aged hands into his slacks, pressing his white lab coat back from a lean frame. "From what little time

I've had to examine the bones, I've been able to fill in some blanks. Late twenties, maybe edging into his thirties. I can't tell you how long he's been out there under the extreme conditions of the park for sure, but I can tell you there are several breaks in his legs that are consistent with a fall from a great height. I have little hope this set of bones is connected to your current missing person investigation. Not only from the difference in victimology but also the condition of the remains. These bones weren't presented as a statement. I think they were just in the vicinity."

Simpson seemed to stiffen at Callen's side, drawing himself taller. His voice dropped an octave. "You said you're waiting for confirmation on his identity. Do you have a suspicion of who he might be?"

"There have only been a handful of missing persons reported in Zion, Ranger Simpson." A knowing expression turned down the corners of the ME's eyes, but he held himself confident. "Only two in the last five years. One of those being your brother."

The air seemed to suction out of the room.

Simpson's brother had gone missing? All this time Callen had been collaborating with the law enforcement ranger to find Lauren, and the man standing next to him had lost his own sibling in this damn park?

"You think this is Jackson?"

"His height, age markers and bearing match those of Jackson Simpson, yes. As I said, I was able to gather X-rays before your arrival. Our best shot of identifying him is to compare these teeth to your brother's dental records. I should have confirmation within a couple of days." Dr. Yarrow really did look sympathetic then. It wasn't the automated response of a man who worked solely with the dead and their families armed with unending questions, a man just doing his job to move on to the next case. Real sympathy laced his tone. “I’m sorry, Ranger Simpson. I wish I had better news.”

Simpson scrubbed one hand down his face, his eyes glued to the bones spread in a broken puzzle across the table. “I’ve got to make a call. Excuse me.”

A tingling sensation built in Callen’s toes and fingers, similar to the lack of oxygen he’d felt while fighting for his life in the Virgin River, and all he could think to do was cut his attention to Maeve. To feel her grounding presence as his own grief charged forward. A reminder that while he’d spent an entire year searching for some sign his sister was still alive, he’d gotten what he’d wanted in the end: to bring Lauren home. Callen cleared his throat. “You wouldn’t happen to have confirmation on the identity of the first set of remains, would you, Dr. Yarrow?”

“I do. It seems whoever tried to kill you and shot your partner here was telling the truth. Dental records were a one hundred percent match as the bones had been well taken care of. She is Lauren Russell.” The medical examiner’s lips pursed as he considered Maeve.

She hadn’t moved, didn’t even seem to breathe under his assessment.

“When will her remains be released?” Callen licked dry lips, dreading all the little conversations and details he’d have to discuss with his parents. “My family… They’re in town. They’ll want to take her home to Salt Lake, have an official funeral, say goodbye.”

The missing piece to their family had been recovered,

but Callen didn't feel any more whole. There were still too many questions unanswered. Too many possibilities of another threat. To him. To Maeve. The killer had accused Callen of standing in his way of what he wanted, but Callen had no intention of letting the bastard through.

Maeve reached for his hand, smoothing circles into the space between his thumb and index finger as he had the night she'd woken from her nightmare, and the muscles along his shoulders loosened. She'd done that. Chased back the tension he'd held on to for months in searching for Lauren, interviewing everyone who'd ever come in contact with his sister, going through her personal things and her apartment. She grounded him in a way no one else could, and he loved her for it.

Hell. Was still in love with her.

His body temperature hiked up a few more degrees as the truth settled in his gut. From the moment she'd set foot on that trail, he'd been drawn in. By her. The care she'd shown his parents, the dedication and loyalty she'd proven to have for Lauren, the personal sacrifice she'd made to come here to Zion and fix what had become broken. He had no reason to believe she'd want anything to do with him after this investigation concluded, but Callen wasn't selfless enough to let her walk out of his life again without facing this familiar pull between them. He didn't know what it would take, but he wasn't willing to give up this time. Not after everything they'd been through.

"As much as I want to be able to tell you I can release your sister's remains now, I understand there's another missing young woman you're searching for in connection to her death." The ME rose onto his toes, then rocked back on his heels as though they were talking about the damn weather.

Maeve raised those dark eyes to the forensic pathologist, seemingly coming back into the moment. She moved to stand, and Callen was right there, his hands beneath one arm. "Her name is Iliana Meyer. She's a forensic analyst out of Vegas. We believe she was abducted by the same person responsible for Lauren's disappearance."

"Right. Iliana Meyer. You mentioned her last time we talked, but I haven't seen any updates from her investigation come through." The medical examiner crossed toward his desk, pulling a pair of glasses from his lab coat front pocket and setting them on his nose. Glancing over the brim, he tapped in his password on one of the oldest desktop computers Callen had ever seen. "This is a current case Springdale PD is working, right? Who is the detective who asked you to consult?"

"I don't remember his name." Maeve's hand clamped around his, her mouth flattening into a straight line. She wasn't supposed to leave the hospital for a few more days. She'd most likely overdone it and was paying the price every minute her stubbornness won. A thin film of sweat sheened along her temple. He had to get her back to the hospital. "Iliana's vehicle was recovered last week, but there wasn't any DNA or prints left in the car, from what I understand. Police have already released the scene, and without any significant leads, it's possible Springdale PD has shuffled the case to the bottom of their priority list. The victims disappeared over a year apart. They might not have made the connection at all."

"Oh, I imagine they did if they asked you to join the investigation. Let's take a look." Shaking his head, Dr. Yarrow pinched his eyebrows together as he read the screen from a standing position. "Looks like Detective Ike is the lead, but that's odd. I don't see the Taser you brought in to fingerprint cataloged in the evidence section of the file."

Maeve shuffled away from her chair, heading for the door. "Ike. That's right. I remember now. Things have been a bit fuzzy the past few days."

"In case you haven't heard, Agent Perry was shot four days ago." Callen tightened his hold on Maeve's hand, helping her toward the door. Her pulse pounded into the palm of his hand. She was overexerting herself, but he'd known trying to keep her from coming to the morgue would've only ended in her sneaking out of the hospital alone. Wounded. Vulnerable.

"Well, now that we suspect these newest remains don't have anything to do with your investigation into your missing person, I'll reach out to Captain Hendricks at Springdale PD and let him know." The ME drew his glasses from his face, biting the end of one earpiece. "Can I also assume you'll be filing the evidence with him once you're recovered?"

Maeve's smile didn't reach her eyes. "Of course."

"One more thing, Ms. Perry. I understand you've been through a trauma these past few days, so I don't want you to worry about the fingerprint results you ran the other day." Dr. Yarrow pointed the tip of his glasses at Maeve. "I took the liberty of forwarding them Springdale PD. In fact, both Detective Ike and the captain are very interested in discussing why you're working the Iliana Meyer case."

Maeve's grip tightened on his hand, just slightly.

What the hell? Callen didn't understand. "What are you talking about? Springdale PD invited her to consult because of her connection to the original investigation last year."

"Did they? Because I reached out to the FBI's Las Vegas office and spoke with the special agent in charge there." Dr. Yarrow shifted his gaze to the woman at Callen's side. "And he told me Maeve Perry is not one of their agents."

Chapter Twenty-Two

Too soon. This was all happening too soon.

Maeve couldn't feel the warmth from Callen's hand anymore, as though some part of her was already shutting down. She'd known the truth would come out. But she should've had more time. And she didn't even blame Dr. Yarrow. He was protecting his case the best he knew how. By exposing her.

Callen slipped his hand from hers, leaving her to stand on her own two feet. "What the hell is he talking about? Why would the Vegas office say you're not one of their agents?"

Her heart pounded hard. Too hard and too fast. To the point she wasn't sure Callen couldn't hear it from where he stood. Maeve tried to straighten, but the sutures made that impossible. "I can explain."

Dark eyes leveled on her, and suddenly she was right back on the Kolob Arch trail, seeing him for the first time in over a year. Seeing the hatred and the anger and the blame in his gaze. His words barely reached over the buzz coming from the wall of refrigerators, from where she assumed Lauren's remains—though stripped of anything needing to be preserved—waited to be taken home to Salt Lake. "What did you do?"

Maeve's gaze darted to Dr. Yarrow. The medical examiner had given her access to his equipment and workspace based on her word and outdated credentials. She'd lied to him—to Callen—but there hadn't been any other option. Pressing a hand to her stomach, she tried holding herself together. In vain. Whatever remnants of their relationship she and Callen had revived wouldn't survive, but she had to try. "Springdale PD gave up on Lauren in less than two months after she disappeared with no new leads, but I couldn't leave her out here. I couldn't stop. I made a promise to bring her home, and I was going to do everything I could to keep that promise."

Maeve tried to relieve the pressure in her gut, shifting her weight between both feet, but the heaviness had nothing to do with her posture. It came from the hard lines sharpening in Callen's expression. "But after that notebook went missing from my hotel room, my superiors called me back to Salt Lake. They learned about my personal connection to Lauren and suspended me from working the investigation. I should've been fired then, but my case history saved me. I didn't… I didn't tell you because you were already dealing with so much. I didn't want to add to your grief or take away from what you needed. So I pushed it all down to deal with later, but then you asked me for an update on the investigation, and I didn't know what to say. I couldn't lie to you. You deserved to know I'd been removed from the case, and then we broke up, and I… My job was all I had, and my career was on thin ice. Until I was injured in the field."

It took everything she had not to sink at the pure vitriol carved into Callen's expression. A sick feeling swirled through her as he stared down at her. His mother had told him the details, but the slight tremor in his hands revealed how much he hadn't known, that it affected him. Her jaw ached under the pressure of her clenched teeth as everything she'd tried to bury at the back of her mind slipped free. "According to the psychologist I was ordered to meet with after I was released from the hospital, I was no longer fit for duty. Mentally or physically. So I was suspended from the FBI."

The tendons in Callen's neck bulged as he took a step toward her. Not once since she'd met him had he used his size and intensity to intimidate her, but Maeve couldn't help but step back. He wouldn't hurt her. She knew that. But a tendril of anxiety burned through her at not being at full strength from the shooting. "So transferring to the Vegas office after you moved out, being called in to collaborate with Springdale PD—it was all a lie? Is Iliana Meyer even missing, or was that just an excuse for you to show back up in my life?"

Her mouth parted. Did he really think so little of her? Maeve already had her answer. Had she given him any reason not to? "Iliana is missing. She disappeared under the same circumstances as Lauren. I never lied about that."

"No. You just lied about everything else." He shook his head, not even willing to look her in the eye at this point, and that hurt more than Dr. Yarrow exposing her for the liar she was. Hurt more than the sutures pulling at the edges of her skin in an attempt to keep her insides where they belonged.

The past few days hadn't been the reunion she'd imagined, but she and Callen had come to an understanding since she'd faced him on that trail. It was brittle and still had a lot of cracks, but those cracks weren't the fissures they once were. He'd held her during her nightmare, kissed her as though he'd never stopped giving a damn about her and fought to keep her conscious while she bled out. He'd ordered his brother to watch over her in the hospital because he'd been at her side for days and needed the break. In the blink of an eye, he'd smoothed over the rough patches still left on her heart and made her feel wanted. Loved.

And she'd fallen for it. Fallen for him all over again.

"Springdale PD doesn't have the manpower or the resources to keep searching for her. I do. I still have the inheritance, and since I'm not tied to any agency, I can go wherever the case takes me." Maeve reached for him, needing that connection, needed to believe that she could still fix this. That was all she'd ever wanted since losing Lauren's notebook. To make this right. "I can find her. Just like I found Lauren—"

"You didn't find Lauren." Callen dodged her attempt to touch him. "Her killer left her on that trail to get your attention. To get to you. Don't you realize that? All of this—her death, Iliana's disappearance, the killer zip-tying me to the steering wheel before driving my truck into the Virgin River, even that bullet the surgeons pulled out of you. It's all tied back to you. My sister is dead because of you, Maeve."

She couldn't hold back the flinch cutting through her as though he'd physically taken a blade and carved her up. Couldn't deny anything he'd said. It was true. All of it. Everything the killer had done was for one purpose and one purpose only: He wanted her. And Lauren, Iliana, Callen, they were the ones paying the price.

"Do you even realize what you've put at risk?" His question was more growl than words. "Everything we've learned about Lauren's disappearance and murder, everything that might lead us to recovering Iliana Meyer, is inadmissible in court, Maeve. None of it will be considered evidence because you lied about being an agent. The chain of custody on any evidence, including that Taser you found at the scene, is broken. Any prosecutor worth their salt will tear apart this investigation before it even starts. Because of you. Because you compromised it. Again."

Her throat tightened, cutting off her air supply. Blood rushed into her face and neck, her eyes stinging. He was right. How could she have been so blinded by the promise she'd made to his family to not even see history repeating itself? "I wanted to fix it."

"But you didn't. You made things worse, and now we might never find out what really happened to Lauren." Callen threaded a hand through his hair, wrenching his attention to the medical examiner she'd forgotten was there. "You have my number?"

Dr. Yarrow nodded. "I'll contact you as soon as I can release your sister's remains."

"Thanks." Callen didn't bother looking at Maeve as he maneuvered past her and toward the exit leading to the stairs to the funeral home above.

Maeve could only follow him through the morgue's heavy double doors on his heels, barely dodging the swing as they started closing behind him. The temperature climbed a few degrees as she left the examination room behind, but her insides were still cold. "Where are you going?"

"Home." He ascended the first couple of stairs. "I need

to tell my parents not to expect the release of Lauren's remains anytime soon."

Guilt surged like morning acid reflux. The ME had told her Springdale PD was interested in discussing her involvement in the case, which would only slow their search for Iliana. And without any solid evidence connecting the cases of two missing women, there was a chance Lauren might not ever be able to come home. She grabbed for the railing to haul herself up after him, but it would be hard to keep pace. Still, they couldn't leave things like this. She couldn't go another year knowing she'd failed him. "Callen—"

"Don't, Maeve." He turned on her then, stepping down into her personal space. "We're done. You're so hell-bent on doing things yourself, find your own way back to the hospital. You're bleeding through your shirt."

Done? Maeve backed down the two stairs she'd managed to climb, doing everything in her power to stay on her own two feet. Her heart stuttered in her chest. No. He didn't understand. She could still fix this. She could keep her promise to Cieron and his parents, and things would go back to the way they were supposed to. Before Lauren had gone missing. She didn't have any other choice. She didn't have anyone else.

But she couldn't say that. She couldn't stop him from ascending the rest of the stairs and shoving through the door sectioning off the morgue from the funeral home. Before she had a chance to process what'd happened in the past few minutes, Callen was gone.

And for the first time in over a year, she didn't know what to do. Everything she'd done, everything she'd given up, had fallen short. Tendrils of cold worked through her clothing despite the heavy metal doors doing their job to keep the refrigeration where it belonged on the other side. She couldn't stay here, and she doubted Dr. Yarrow would welcome her presence a minute longer, considering she'd lied to him about her connection to Springdale PD and the investigation.

And Callen had been right. Blood seeped through her shirt. Then the pain spread, almost waiting for her acknowledgment before it stole the air from her lungs. She had to go back to the hospital to assess the damage, but the idea of getting there on her own sucked the strength from her legs. Callen wasn't coming back. Those final two words had hammered the last nail into the coffin that was their relationship, but if she gave it any more thought, she might never leave this basement.

Maeve wrapped her hand around the stair railing and pushed one foot in front of the other. One step at a time, holding her breath when the pain got to be too much and moaning to an empty stairwell between attempts. Until she reached the main floor. The funeral home itself was dark, lit with nothing but backup lighting. The front double glass doors closed behind her as she stepped free of the freezing interior. Night had fallen sometime in the past couple of hours, isolating her further.

She'd only paid for a couple nights at the motel. Her belongings had probably been tossed in the nearest dumpster, her laptop sold or stolen and her car towed from the lot. Extracting her phone, Maeve tapped the contacts app to call for a ride. She hovered over the meager list. Helen. Tommy. Cieron. Callen. People who'd once been her family. She wasn't so sure that was the case anymore, and a sob threatened to break free.

The sound of shuffling tugged at her attention from behind.

She turned to face the interruption, just as lightning exploded across her skull.

Chapter Twenty-Three

She'd lied to him. Again.

Maeve had kept vital information from him concerning the investigation around his sister's disappearance, and he'd been blind to it the entire time. The fact that she hadn't carried her sidearm into the park, that she didn't seem to be in contact with anyone but the law enforcement rangers, that she'd gone out of her way to Hurricane to process the fingerprints on the Taser recovered at the scene of both disappearances. No missed calls or check-in messages with a partner. No collaboration with Springdale PD investigators. Hell, even her thorough search of the latest crime scene where he'd assumed she'd already been twisted into a new light. She'd walked that riverbank as though she'd never been there. Because she hadn't. Everything—from the moment she'd shown her face at Kolob Arch to her standing at the bottom of that stairwell, looking up at him—had been a complicated game she'd put into play.

And he'd fallen for it. Fallen for her.

In a matter of days, she'd worked her way back into his life and beneath his skin, and he'd welcomed it. Wanted it. Dreaded her leaving when the case concluded. This case had sparked something in him. Not just due to the lead she'd uncovered at the river or that his sister's killer had felt threatened enough to show himself after a year of dead ends, but because Maeve had been right here. Within reach.

Turned out, that dread had been misplaced. She wouldn't have gone back to Vegas when the investigation ended because she hadn't transferred to that office to begin with. Her career with the FBI had ended mere days after they'd broken up—another piece of the puzzle she'd kept to herself—and he couldn't help but feel responsible for that. For what she'd suffered. He'd forced her hand by asking her to step into Lauren's investigation—a case neither she nor the FBI should've had any jurisdiction in—and when the entire case had fallen apart, Maeve had taken the punishment without telling him. To protect him.

But that didn't make up for what she'd done. Because now there would be no additional support to continue the search for Iliana Meyer, no resources Springdale PD hadn't already used up, and no justice for Lauren or this latest victim. Maeve had made sure of that.

Callen wrung both hands around the SUV's steering wheel. With his truck still at the bottom of the Virgin River until police managed to get the equipment they needed to haul it out, he was stuck driving back to Springdale in one of the park's vehicles. Inky velvet blackness consumed both sides of the freeway as Hurricane dimmed in the rearview mirror.

What promise had she made to bring Lauren home? To whom? His mom? And why hadn't Maeve told him the truth from the beginning? Why did she feel the need to keep everything so close to the vest? He could've helped her. He would have, knowing Maeve was doing this all for his family. Except…he'd cut off all contact with her after the breakup. Ignored her calls and messages, then blocked and deleted her number when the temptation to answer became too much. He hadn't given her the chance to ask for help.

Hell. None of it mattered. It wasn't like he'd see her again. He'd meant what he said. They were done. There wasn't a single cell in his body that wanted to face her again after her lies had come to light. She'd compromised Lauren's investigation all over again. Only this time, another victim would pay the price.

"Damn it." All he'd ever wanted was to keep his family from falling apart. But by allowing the one person who'd recovered the first real piece of evidence in over a year back into his life, he'd destroyed any chances of success. He didn't know what he was going to say to his parents. How he would explain what Maeve had done. Their daughter was currently resting in a funeral home basement masquerading as a morgue, and she would stay there until someone who didn't even know Lauren decided to let her go. For how long? Days? Weeks? Months? Another year? How was he supposed to tell his mother she had to keep waiting? That the woman she and his father had once seen as a daughter in her own right had ruined their chances of getting the closure they deserved?

Maeve had justified her actions by laying the blame for lack of progress in his sister's case at Springdale PD's feet, and maybe she was right in that regard. Manpower, funding, priority—these were things every police department had to work through to get results, but it was the victims who suffered in the end. It was Iliana Meyer who would be the one to suffer. Because the shooter was still out there, targeting people he believed to be in the way of getting what he really wanted: Maeve.

Callen scrubbed one hand down his face, catching the edge of the massive bruise on the left side of his head where he'd slammed into the driver's-side window as his truck was tossed downriver like a child's plaything. Exhaustion blurred the oncoming headlights coming from the other side of the freeway. He'd be back in Springdale in twenty minutes, give or take, but every mile felt neverending, leaving him with nothing but his thoughts. His accusations.

If Maeve had just done her job right the first time—logging Lauren's notebook from the scene of her disappearance into evidence that night—none of this would've happened. Iliana Meyer never would've been taken. Callen wouldn't have nearly drowned. And Maeve...wouldn't have been shot throwing herself in front of a bullet meant for him.

His throat dried. He could still feel the warmth leech from her body as he held her on that riverbank, swore that no matter how many times he scrubbed his hands her blood remained under his fingernails. And he'd left her back in that stairwell still bleeding. Her face and hands had been so pale, her legs practically shaking from the effort it took to remain upright, but learning the truth had cut him off from feeling any kind of sympathy. He was just so angry. At Maeve for compromising the case, at the man who'd tried to kill him in the first place, at Lauren for leaving, at his parents for not needing him, at Cieron for throwing his life away on drugs and alcohol and who knew what else instead of facing the truth. Lauren was gone. Their baby sister was gone, and no amount of coping mechanisms was going to change that.

His head pulsed in rhythm to his racing heartbeat. That anger burned as though he'd caught fire, and he didn't know how to make it go away. Callen twisted the steering wheel, and he slammed on the brakes. A dust cloud kicked up all along the SUV as he skidded to a stop on the side of the road. Cars he didn't really see shot past as he stared out the windshield, his head wrapped up in the moment he was sure Maeve had taken her last breath on that riverbank.

The stillness and silence that'd descended, as though the entire world had come to a full stop, the lack of life in her features, the way his entire body had become numb as he stared down at her. And all he'd been able to think about was that they hadn't had enough time. He'd thought he'd known heartbreak when Lauren had gone missing, then when he and Maeve had separated. He'd been an idiot.

An inhuman roar filled the interior of the SUV, shocking him back into the moment. Raw pain clawed up his throat, and only then did he realize the sound had come from him. His knuckles strained against the backs of his hands and stretched the lacerated skin around his wrists.

She'd died. In his arms on that riverbank. Maeve had died, and he'd ignored the hollowness in his chest that said a piece of him had died right along with her for days. But he couldn't ignore it anymore. He couldn't ignore the grief and the rage from losing his sister anymore. Couldn't hide behind that anger of watching his brother fade year after year anymore, of watching his parents succumb to the sorrow and pain of losing a child.

It'd all tangled into thin knots he was sure he could handle, and he had for the most part. One by one, he'd faced trying to get Cieron into a program that stuck, taking care of things around his parents' house when he came up to see them so they didn't have to, remembering birthdays and anniversaries and arranging family dinners when he got into town. He sent Christmas presents and made weekly calls while not expecting a damn thing in return from the people who relied on him, but it hadn't been enough. He hadn't been enough as all those strings combined into a vise that left him breathless and sometimes a stranger in his own body. As he stared at the ceiling in his bedroom night after night as though the damn thing could provide answers.

And all those strings? They'd stemmed from the same source: guilt. From not being able to help his sister, for ending things between him and Maeve the way he had, and from failing his parents in every way that mattered. He'd ruined the most important and fulfilling relationship he'd ever had—something that'd been solely selfish and undeserving—by taking out his anger on Maeve when it should've been on him from the start. But Callen shut it down. He shut it all down as he pressed his back into the driver's seat, out of breath as though he'd sprinted the last twenty miles.

He'd left her.

Maeve had been standing at the bottom of those stairs, asking him to understand why she'd lied, and he'd left her there. Bleeding. Weak. Vulnerable. Heat that had nothing to do with the warm air blowing through the vents ticked up his body temperature. He wasn't this man. At least, he didn't used to be. Right? He'd helped build an entire empire on protecting those who couldn't protect themselves, and he'd left Maeve open to the threat that was still out there. To fight alone. Told her to make her way back to the hospital on her own. How could he have done that to her? How could she ever forgive him?

Callen checked over his shoulder, hauling the steering wheel in a tight turn. There was no official crossing between both halves of the freeway highway patrol liked to use to catch speeders, but he didn't care. The SUV could handle a little off-roading. Clear from potentially T-boning another vehicle, he slammed his foot against the accelerator and dropped the SUV into the desert gap and jerked onto the southbound lanes.

One minute. Five. Fifteen. The lights peppering the small town of Hurricane became clearer with each passing minute. Time seemed to have sped up now that he had a purpose again: getting to Maeve.

Maneuvering into the Metland Funeral Home's semicircular driveway much too fast, Callen clipped the curb and shoved the SUV into Park. He shouldered free of the vehicle and rounded the hood before sprinting for the glass double doors. He jerked the door toward him. "Son of a bitch."

Locked. He pressed both hands around his eyes, filtering out the streetlights to search through the doors. It was dark, with no sign of movement. Backing up, Callen studied the windows framed with black shutters on either side of the door and noted the security sensors. Dr. Yarrow might still be inside, but he doubted it. It was well past the ME's operating hours. He knocked on the glass. Just in case. "Maeve!"

He stepped into the bushes to test the nearest window.

Glass crunched beneath the sole of his boot. A nearby streetlight cast a dull yellow glow across the screen of a broken phone. Dread pooled at the base of his spine as Callen collected the device. A familiar photo lit up through the cracked screen as he raised it.

Of him and Maeve taken the night he'd asked her to marry him.

She'd kept it as her background all this time? The screen darkened as it tried to read his face to grant him access and failed, and he tipped Maeve's phone down. Catching sight of the dark stain spread across the pavement. That hadn't been there when he'd left. Crouching, Callen swiped his index and middle fingers through the thickest rim of liquid.

Coming away with fresh blood.

Chapter Twenty-Four

Was she dead yet?

She kinda wanted to be, with that gut-wrenching drumbeat in her head.

Maeve turned her head to one side, some kind of hard surface digging into her skull. Didn't help the explosion of pain radiating from the back of her head either. Cracking her eyes, she flinched against the bare light bulb slightly swinging above her head, blocking out the rest of what smelled like a basement torture chamber. Okay. She might not be dead yet, but based on the scarred wood table supporting her and the serial killer vibes, she wasn't sure she should've woken up. She tried to drag one hand up. Zip-tied to one of the table legs. Same with the other hand and both ankles. Her abductor had done his job well in making sure she couldn't star in one of those cheesy horror films by running upstairs and into a dead end as the killer gave pursuit. "You've got to be kidding me."

A defeated laugh kicked at her ribs. Because there was only one person she could think of who would want to restrain her, murder-style, and she didn't have the time or the patience to play this game. Not with Iliana still missing, with Callen having to inform his parents of what she'd done and her head screaming. Warmth soaked through her shirt, an all-too-familiar feeling she wished she could stop experiencing. Then there was her gunshot wound. Bleeding out the first time hadn't been a picnic, and she was willing to bet this time wouldn't be a roll in the hay either. Tipping her chin to her chest, Maeve tried to gauge the damage, but without being able to move her shirt out of the way, there was no telling how much blood she'd lost or whether the wound was still leaking. "Just my luck. I'm going to bleed out on a torture table before my captor even has the chance to reveal himself and answer all my questions."

Rude.

"I tried to stop the bleeding." Movement sounded from off to her right, but she couldn't distinguish shadow from where the ring of light from the bulb overhead ended. "But to be honest, I'm probably the last person who should be poking around a gunshot wound."

Setting her head back against the table, Maeve stared up at the bulb covered in thin wisps of cobwebs. Not only did she have to worry about dying, but spiders too. Great. "Considering you put it there, seems only fair you be the one to fix it."

"You've always been funny, Maeve. That's one of the things I love about you." Love seemed like a strong word coming from a man who'd tried to kill her and Callen—who possibly killed Lauren and contributed to Iliana's disappearance—but who was she to judge? "Even after your dad died, you went out of your way to make sure everyone else could still paste a smile on their face with funny stories of him at that reception. No one ever noticed you weren't smiling, though. No one but me, that is."

That...wasn't possible. She'd known every single person who'd come to the house after the funeral, even her father's work friends, his extended family and the neighbors. Whoever had killed Lauren wasn't one of them. Maeve shook her head, splinters from the table digging into the sensitive skin of her scalp. She remembered those stories, the ones that'd always gotten a good laugh out of Callen and the Russells when she'd told them. There was no way this man had heard them. "You weren't there."

"Of course I was. I was invited." He stepped just outside the weak circle of light caressing the limits of the table, gloved hands leveraged against the edge as he bent over her. Stains marred the black leather, hints of something metallic coating the back of her throat and tongue. Blood.

It'd taken her a few moments to process what he'd said. He'd *tried* to stop the bleeding. Other details of the room came into focus then. The discarded paper wrappers just past his legs, the bloodied squares of gauze strewn near what looked to be a wooden wall of some kind. No windows to determine where she'd been dragged, but under the thick odor of blood—her blood—was something dry and fresh. Cold. The room itself was cold. "Where am I?"

"Right where you belong, sweetheart." Her abductor rounded the table near her feet, and her defenses kicked into high gear. It'd been bad enough he'd put those hands on her to try to staunch the bleeding, but she couldn't protect herself from his position now. A strategy she was sure he'd thought of exactly for that reason. "With me."

But for how long? How long did she have until her body gave up? Tugging on the zip ties, she tried to keep her expression neutral as the plastic bit into the skin around her wrists. As it had while Callen struggled to escape the truck. It'd been a matter of not having the right angle for him, but Maeve had the distinct impression it would be the same for her now. There was little slack between the zip ties at her wrists and whatever they'd been secured to on the table. A leg, maybe? If she couldn't summon the force to break through the binding.

"Oh, come on now, Maeve. You know I wasn't going to make it that easy for you. I've been waiting a long time to have you all to myself." He was on the move again, glimpses of dark hair peeking out from beneath the black ski mask hiding his features. His voice—it was right there on the tip of her memory. She knew it, didn't she? The slow, drawling way he spoke, the dry humor tagged with the occasional spike in tone. "You're a federal agent after all. Well, a former federal agent, I should say. Just as deadly, but without all the red tape."

Maeve might not know him, but he sure as hell seemed to think he knew her, and that was a little terrifying. She was a trained federal agent, as he'd pointed out, but had she missed a killer staring back at her? A rush of warmth spread down her side. Not warmth. Liquid. Blood pooled beneath her right side, seeping into the grains of the table. Stomach wounds were funny like that. They trickled one minute, then gushed the next. Problem was, there was no way to predict which. Or how much you would lose. She was living on borrowed time. "Where's Iliana?"

"Who?" Her abductor arched his back, hands clasped in front of him. "Oh, is that her name? The forensic lady, right? She helped you with a case that one time. I remember you talking about her, how she single-handedly gave the prosecution a win for your case. You got so excited, I could tell, because your eyes lit up for the first time in a long time. I didn't even know her, and I wanted to thank her for putting that light back in your eyes."

"I don't… I don't understand." Maeve tried to shake her head again, but the rough surface of the table only dug deeper. Or maybe her future murderer had hit her too hard. "I've only told that story to…"

He pressed closer to the table, angling himself over her with his hands secured behind his back. He didn't see her as a threat, and that pissed her off more than the possibility that she knew this man. It was impossible to tell his age or height with the mask and dark clothing, but there had to be something—anything—she could use to get ahead of whatever game he'd set into motion. Because she couldn't afford the distraction. "To answer your question, your friend isn't here. She served her purpose. Bringing you to me."

Served. Past tense. Tears burned in her eyes.

"Ah, now, don't be sad." He reached for her, skimming one gloved hand down her shin and leaving a wake of disgust in its place. "I gave her the best death I knew how. I give you my word. She didn't even see it coming."

"When?" She could barely form the word, her mouth was so dry, pained. Coated in failure and remorse and guilt. She hadn't known Iliana Meyer long, but Maeve could attribute the jump in success of her career to the forensic analyst who'd only wanted justice for those who didn't have their voices anymore. "How long ago?"

The mask shifted as though the bastard was smiling down at her. "The same day her vehicle was recovered at the river. Though her bones aren't quite ready for their debut. I'll need a couple more days to get the stains out."

No. Denial surged, choking and hot and suffocating. *No.* "Why?"

"I told you. She served a purpose." Lean shoulders rose and deflated on a shrug. He wasn't as muscular as Callen, maybe as tall, but from this angle, it was hard for Maeve to tell. Scanning her from head to toe, he moved as though they had all the time in the world. But if he kept dragging this out, she'd never get her answers before the wound in her gut claimed her. "Just as Lauren served her purpose."

Maeve looked up. "What?"

"I warned her to keep her mouth shut, but that woman didn't know when to stop." Rounding the head of the table, her abductor—Lauren's and Iliana's killer—positioned himself above her head, and she liked that even less than having him by her feet. "You know, she had this way of getting everything that she wanted without even trying, even at the very end. She didn't like that I wanted you. Tried to talk me out of removing Callen from the equation. Said it was wrong, that I needed help." His laugh felt thick and wrong and sickening. "She was still spewing that crap. Right up until I dragged my blade across her neck."

A whimper left her without permission. For over a year, she'd wanted to know what'd happened to her best friend—the woman who'd helped her learn to accept a new family—but this… She wasn't prepared for this. Dozens of serial cases, upward of forty victims, but Lauren was gone. Maeve dragged her heels up the table to curl in on herself, but the zip ties held her in place.

One gloved hand caressed the side of her neck, the supple leather almost comforting if it didn't belong to the hand of the man responsible for murdering the people she cared about. "He never deserved you. You know that, right? All it took was me taking that notebook from your hotel room to show you that."

She sucked in a shallow, pain-filled—

Wait. What? Her insides coiled tighter, constricting around the bullet wound, and another gush of blood escaped. Maeve blinked as her vision wavered. The edges around her eyes were darker somehow. Was the bulb overhead giving out? Or was her brain playing tricks on her? Because she couldn't have heard him right. "You took… You?"

The notebook. Lauren's notebook. The one piece of evidence that may have helped her find Callen's sister sooner. He'd taken it from her hotel room? He'd ended her career? He'd ended her relationship with Callen? For what? To have her bleed out on this torture table? "How?"

"Well, I couldn't very well leave it behind, considering she'd written so many good things in there about me." He dropped his elbows onto the table, getting that much closer to her. "You know, conversations where I told her how much I was in love with you and that I was going to kill Callen, and how she tried to talk me out of it. Turns out, she was building a little case to have me committed in that annoying secret language you two made up as teens. Only I didn't realize what was in that notebook of hers until you talked yourself into the investigation. I knew it was only a matter of time before you realized what my sister had written, and I couldn't have that."

Her mouth dried. "Sister."

She couldn't think.

Couldn't breathe.

As Cieron Russell removed the ski mask. "Surprise."

Chapter Twenty-Five

The blood trail cut short at the parking lot behind the funeral home.

Callen gripped the flashlight he'd collected from the glove compartment of the SUV until the plastic protested. He didn't have any proof that the blood that'd seeped onto the sidewalk at the front door belonged to Maeve, but his instincts edged him into near desperation. That stain hadn't been there when he'd left. Maeve had had her phone tucked in her back pocket in the morgue.

He could almost convince himself that she'd collapsed from reopening her wound and a Good Samaritan or Dr. Yarrow had called emergency services to intervene. But the dark spotted trail curved toward the back of the building. To an empty parking lot. Not the curving driveway that would've gotten an ambulance closer to her.

Which meant Maeve had been taken.

Only one person would have reason to ambush her.

The killer had finally gotten what he'd wanted.

Callen had left her unprotected, vulnerable, bleeding. Hell, she wouldn't have had the energy to fight back after coming up from the basement. Or maybe he'd surprised her from behind. It didn't matter. What mattered was getting her back. Fixing this.

Jogging back to his SUV, he hauled himself behind the steering wheel and punched the accelerator, tearing down the driveway. He fishtailed back onto the freeway in front of another car, nearly colliding into the back of a smaller sedan as his phone connected to the only person experienced enough to find Maeve before she disappeared like the others. Like Lauren.

Acid burned in his throat as the other line picked up. "Simpson."

"Maeve is missing." Three words. The dam holding him together cracked just a little more, but he couldn't let it break. Not now. Not while Maeve needed him to be strong for her. To bring her home.

Silence beat through the line. One second. Two. "Give me the details."

Callen recalled everything he'd found at the scene of the funeral home and the time between when he'd left Maeve in that cold, empty basement and discovering her phone. "She's injured. Last I checked, she may have torn through one or two of her sutures. There was a lot of blood. I traced it to the back of the building. He must've gotten her into a car. The trail ended at the sidewalk."

"Hurricane PD is on the way. I'll reach out to Dr. Yarrow to meet them and pull Springdale PD in for the search." Simpson didn't miss a beat. "Where would he have taken her?"

"I don't… I don't know." And that was what scared him the most. Not that Maeve couldn't protect herself. She was better trained than some of the men in his security team, but her injuries would slow her down. And finding her in time? He blinked against the oncoming headlights. A patrol cruiser with its lights on—possibly highway patrol—screamed past, heading straight into Hurricane. Callen couldn't think clearly. The possibilities were endless. The killer's previous victims had been nothing but tools to draw Maeve in, to gain her attention. So their vehicles had been left in a public place. Lauren's remains had been left on the trail, easy to find, as Callen's death was meant to be. Public. But he had the feeling that wasn't what the bastard wanted now. The man in the mask had set his plans in motion over a year ago, striking from the shadows, potentially even putting himself in Maeve's life to get closer. He would want to take her somewhere he could take his time, enjoy bending her to his will. "Both Lauren's and Iliana Meyer's vehicles were abandoned at the riverbank, but Maeve doesn't have her car. He had to have taken her in his own vehicle. I searched the area around the funeral home. There are no burnout marks left behind in the parking lot, which means he wasn't in a hurry."

"All right. Well, knowing what I do of Agent Perry and the gaps you've filled in, it's easy to imagine she was probably unconscious when he abducted her. He probably didn't want to have to hurt her." Simpson was on the move, his breath coming in shorter gasps. Running. "That gives me hope she'll be able to fight her way out if necessary. I have three rangers available to aid the search, but I need someplace for them to start."

"Kolob Arch." The words left his mouth without hesitation. "That's where this started. That's where he left Lauren for us to find. He did it to get her attention, but I think there's a reason he chose that location. There's something there he considers important."

Hours and hours of Maeve's rambling when it came

to serial offenders had sunk in over the years. From the time she'd come across her first serial case in college to the last couple of investigations she'd worked before their breakup, there'd been a genuine excitement in her voice with each clue revealed. She'd been fascinated with the serial mind and had wanted him to be as excited. It was those moments, of her studying at their small two-person kitchen table with notebooks and textbooks and her tablet spread across the surface, he remembered most. Not so much the words, but her awe, though some of her words too. Like the fact serial offenders rarely chose their stage at random. They weren't impulsive. They could control themselves, and Callen didn't believe for one second Kolob Arch didn't hold some kind of significance for the shooter who'd taken Maeve.

"And if you're wrong?" Simpson's voice had evened out, the whip of a breeze coming through the line. Of the three rangers the law enforcement division head had said were available to start the search, Callen was betting the man had included himself. And then Callen was reminded of that reason, of how there was a second set of remains stored in one of those refrigerators in the basement morgue that had the potential to be Simpson's missing brother. While Simpson had possibly found the answers he'd been searching for—for who knew how long—Callen felt the ranger's need to help with miles between them.

The darkness on either side of the freeway seemed to close in, matching the hollowness spreading through his chest. The space where he'd once felt whole pulsed hard enough to still his next breath. He couldn't be wrong. Not when it came to Maeve. But hadn't the past few days shown him exactly how wrong he'd been about her in every regard? From her commitment to the family that'd taken her in to the cost she was willing to pay to make up for the past. She'd held on long after he'd given up on them, and he couldn't swallow the shame and guilt driving him to go faster, get to her quicker. Maeve Perry had given up everything to do what she felt was right—to repay his family and provide them closure—and he'd only punished her for it.

She'd lied to him, led him to believe there would be justice at the end of this investigation, but justice had failed Lauren long before Maeve ever did. Because she was right. Police had given up after mere weeks, just as they'd already given up on Iliana Meyer, but Maeve hadn't. Their half-assed investigation—whether due to low manpower, even lower resources or low priority—hadn't been enough for her. She'd seen his need to have answers, and she'd gone after them with no consideration of herself, her career or the storm she'd be putting herself in by facing him after all this time.

And for that, Callen recognized how much he didn't deserve her. Those tentative smiles when he'd tried verbally cutting her down, the handful of seconds she'd let him hold her after her nightmare, that kiss he'd claimed without thought, her risking her life by dragging him out of that river and taking that bullet so he wouldn't have to.

He hadn't deserved any of it. Hell, he'd even taken it all for granted, but there wouldn't be a single moment he didn't pay her back when he found her. Because he loved her. He'd loved her since the moment they'd finally broken that sibling's-best-friend barrier and she'd hugged him after her father's funeral just to thank him for showing up. A spark had flared that day and hadn't left since, even after she'd moved out. Only now it burned hotter, drove him harder. Maeve was all there was for him. No other woman had come close to easing the grief and emptiness like she did, and he couldn't let her go. Not again. Not ever again.

"I'm not wrong. He'll have taken her to Kolob Arch." Callen funneled the SUV off the freeway, heading directly into Springdale. Maeve didn't have a lot of time, but he wouldn't go in blind. Wouldn't put her at further risk.

"We're headed out now. Meet you there as soon as we can." Simpson ended the call from his end of the line, leaving Callen in a cocoon of silence as he pulled the SUV into his driveway.

His parents' vehicle was parked at the curb. He hadn't had the chance to explain anything since leaving the funeral home that first time, not wanting to talk about Lauren over the phone instead of to their faces, but now wasn't the time. Maeve needed him, and he wasn't going to fail her this time.

Charging through the front door, he noted his parents spread out on the sectional in front of the TV before rushing down the hallway into the second bedroom. Ugh. Looked as though Cieron had made himself more than comfortable for his short stay with the slight hint of odor coming off the walls. His brother hadn't even bothered putting on the fitted sheet or the bedding Callen had pulled from the dryer and laid at the end of the mattress.

"You're late." His mother followed on his heels, hair in the same curlers she'd used since he was a kid and her face clean of makeup. Sweeping her hands in front of her face, she tried to clear the obvious smoke smell, but it wouldn't do a damn bit of good. "I was getting worried something had happened at the hospital. How is Maeve doing?"

Callen's heart stopped for a beat as he tore into the bedroom closet. After his storage container had been broken into, he couldn't leave an entire arsenal open for civilians or the curious to take advantage of. He'd managed to not go insane in the days between getting Maeve to the hospital and when she'd woken by moving most of his weapons and gear here. Now he needed it to find her. He thumbed the keypad of the gun safe at the top of the closet and pulled one of his sidearms free before grabbing a box of ammo and tossing them onto the tangled bed. "I don't know how to answer that."

"What do you mean?" Helen Russell rounded into his peripheral vision, much shorter but so much more intimidating than most women his age. Or maybe that'd come from a lifetime being raised by one of the strongest women he'd known. Her voice notched higher as she dragged on his arm to slow him down. "Callen Russell, tell me what's going on. Right now."

He couldn't keep it from her. Not if this ended with Maeve… He would need her to hold him together, just as she had for those weeks he'd been sick with pneumonia at twelve years old. Callen opened his mouth to answer, taking in Cieron's mess, but stepped deeper into the closet at the sight of something he hadn't seen in over a year.

A bright yellow notebook peeking out from his brother's unzipped overnight bag. Callen crossed the floor in less than two steps.

"Callen?" His mom's concern practically radiated off her. "What's happened?"

He ripped the all-too-familiar notebook free from Cieron's bag and turned to face her. "What is this?"

"I don't know. That's Cieron's bag. I've never seen..." His mother's eyebrows pinched together, then smoothed over in horror. Stumbling back, she held a hand to her chest as the truth registered between them. "No."

Callen held on to his sister's notebook—a notebook Maeve had lost everything over—with a death grip. "Where is he?"

Chapter Twenty-Six

It wasn't possible.

But the face staring down at her wasn't an illusion. The mask had hidden his most striking features, but the eyes… She should've recognized his eyes, a piercing blue that matched his father's rather than the dark intensity of Helen Russell's. "You."

Cieron cocked his head to one side. "Me."

Her bones suddenly felt too big for her body, gravity too heavy on her muscles. "You killed Lauren."

Her almost-brother-in-law—the closest man she'd had to a brother—rounded down the side of the table, setting himself up to her right. "I can tell this is coming as quite a shock for you, so I'll give you a minute."

The change in his positioning didn't do much for the anxiety burning through her. She still couldn't breathe without aggravating the sutures in her still-leaking gut, couldn't force her brain to catch up with reality. Tears she'd swallowed back over and over finally broke that internal barrier she'd summoned since seeing Callen for the first time in a year. "You tried to kill Callen."

"Would have, too, if you weren't so damn determined to save everyone." His wide smile flashed with newly whitened teeth, but she'd seen the truth that night she'd found him in the warehouse. What the drugs had done to him inside and out. "That bullet was never meant for you, but you just couldn't stop yourself from playing hero, Maeve. Never could. I think it's one of the things I love about you. Why I fell in love with you, but no matter how many times I tried to tell you, I couldn't. Because I knew you would never choose me."

Love. No. That…that didn't make sense. Cieron wasn't in love with her. Fisting her hands at her sides, Maeve focused on the sharpness of her nails in her palms rather than the steady drip coming from her stomach. She didn't know what the hell she'd done to tear the sutures, but she'd obviously done more damage than she thought. "Listen to me, Cieron. You don't love me. You just think you do because we've been through hard things together. It happens, and I don't blame you for thinking that night I got you to the hospital was more than what really—"

"Don't patronize me!" Cieron slammed his fist into the wood beside her head, and a ringing started in her ear. Vibrations seemed to tremor through him as he stared down at her with an expression she'd never seen before. Tight and full of rage. This wasn't the man she'd known. The man who'd driven her and Lauren to the movies or to a party their parents didn't know about or bought them their first case of beer had always owned a sly smile that could slay any woman's resistance, a lazy way of moving and sarcasm that ended in laughs. He'd been the perfect brother looking out for them when they got in over their heads as teens, then the fun brother when they'd crossed over the eighteen-year threshold. But this man… she didn't know this man, and Maeve's instincts told her she didn't want to. "I don't have some kind of savior complex, Maeve. Nothing changed for me the night you took me to the emergency room, though I appreciated your help from letting me die and promising to find my sister. Unnecessary but appreciated. I'd already decided long before that night that you would be mine. And now you are."

His. No. She wasn't his, and the longer she remained strapped to this table, the more likely she wasn't leaving whatever hellhole he'd dragged her to. A gust of wind battered the wall behind him, the wood groaning under the force. The entire room felt as though it would crash down around them given the slightest push. She couldn't stay here, but running out into the night blind, with a hole in her stomach, wouldn't be any better for what he had planned. "You don't want to do this. Callen—"

His growl reverberated off the already shaky walls. Cieron planted both hands on the table, on each side of her, leaning in close enough she caught hints of marijuana on his clothing. "Enough about my brother. He's not coming for you, Maeve. I saw him leave you at the funeral home without turning back and drive away. Probably running back to Mommy and Daddy like he always does when things don't go his way. He and Lauren had that in common, as you know. He lost his chance. Now it's my turn, and as soon as I'm done getting what I want from you, I'll finish what I started with him. After all, it's the least he deserves."

Callen. Her vision wavered again. It was getting harder to keep her eyes open, and she really, truly did not want to pass out in the presence of a man who felt entitled to her. Her training directed her to memorize the layout of the small space. The room itself didn't have much in the way of furniture, the table she'd been zip-tied to taking up most of the space, though she was sure it'd been moved from one of the other walls into the center of the shack-like design. No windows. No signs of anyone having lived here. Not a house. Another gust of wind rattled the thin wood door with knots drilled straight through it. A fire extinguisher had been installed on a hook near the hinges with a toolbox and thin sleeping cot off to one side. "And what is it you want from me, Cieron? Why go through all this trouble? Why kill Lauren and Iliana and try to drown your brother?"

"You, Maeve. I just want you. I want you to want me as much as I want you, and if you don't, I want you to hurt as much as I do watching you choose my brother over and over despite how he's treated you." Shoving away from the table, he backed up until he hit what looked like a plain desk. "So what's it going to be?"

"You've already hurt me." She didn't miss the flinch in his shoulders. He didn't like the fact that she was bleeding out. The gunshot wound most likely ruined whatever plans he'd had in bringing her here, but if she was being honest, it was ruining hers too. She wouldn't make it far when she ran. Maeve twisted her left wrist—the one most likely out of his line of vision—until the edge of the zip tie cut through the first layer of skin. This would hurt, but it would be quick once she followed through. She just had to keep him distracted enough not to notice. "You see that, don't you, Cieron? Killing Lauren, abducting Iliana and driving Callen's truck into the river with him inside, the bullet wound. All those things have already hurt me, are still hurting me. You're not supposed to hurt the people you love, and you've hurt me far more than Callen ever has."

Her heart threatened to give under the lie. Because the truth was, Callen had hurt her, but the scars and the wounds weren't visible to the naked eye. They'd cut much deeper. From ending their engagement to the barbs he'd thrown at her over the past few days, she wasn't sure whether there was anything left for her and Callen to salvage. But she wanted there to be. She wanted to tell him how sorry she was that she'd lied, that she hadn't gotten to Lauren in time, that she hadn't seen the threat before now. She wanted him to know she might've taken that bullet to save his life but that he'd saved hers more times than she could count in some of the smallest ways. By ordering takeout for them after an especially hard day in the field, for showing her what it felt like to be wanted when no one else had stepped forward to claim her after her father's death, by hunting down the man who'd destroyed everything she'd known and never shying away from the nightmares that chased her until she woke screaming. Callen had been there to shape her from the moment she'd stepped over the Russells' threshold. He'd trained her to adapt and crawl out onto the other side when things got too overwhelming, and he'd handed her the weapons and the courage to stand her ground against some of the worst threats she'd ever faced.

Breaking her heart, ending their future—neither of those things held a candle to all the good he'd brought into her life. And she wasn't ready to let the darkness win. Not then and not now.

Maeve clenched her jaw against the sharp pain lancing through her as she arched her wrist upward, straining the plastic. All she needed was a little more pressure. What was this place? A shed? No. Nobody installed a fire extinguisher in a storage shed. Well, except for Callen, but his storage container had been different. He'd turned it into an impressive arsenal she could only attribute to him. The man loved his weapons, always wanting to be prepared. But he wouldn't be prepared for this. Things had changed between them, but she had to believe there was still something worth saving from their relationship.

Cieron closed his eyes, and she took her chance, risking the pain. "You forced my hand. I didn't want to hurt them, but you made me. By not seeing I was right there in front of you. By choosing him."

The zip tie snapped, though Maeve didn't give any hint as to the change in her circumstances. "I didn't make you do anything. You're the one who chose to hurt them, Cieron. You're responsible for your actions. Nobody else."

"No!" He charged the table again, quickly losing the short sense of calm. "You did this. You got into my head and refused to leave. Every time I saw you, you paraded yourself in front of me until you were all I could think about, all I could dream about. But you've haunted me long enough."

Reaching to the back of his waistband, Cieron withdrew a blade like the ones she'd seen in Callen's arsenal. Serrated and deadly enough to kill. "Don't worry, Maeve. This won't take long. You're already halfway there, and once you're gone, I'll be sure to pay my brother a visit."

No. "Cieron—"

He arched the knife down.

Maeve snapped her free hand up, stopping the blade a mere inch from her heart. Her mouth parted just as Cieron's eyes widened.

His breath huffed against her jawline, prickling her skin. "What the…"

She didn't give him a chance to recover. Curving the side of her index finger over his knuckles, she made contact with the blade's rough grip and shoved everything she had into turning the sharp end into his gut. The steel cut deep and quick. Lodging in his stomach. Grief that had no business surfacing flooded through her. "I'm sorry."

His laugh rumbled from the half-cocked smile she'd come to love. "No, you're not, but that's okay. You will be."

She didn't understand his meaning but couldn't risk giving him another opportunity to strike. Tugging the bloody metal from his gut, she ignored Cieron's stumble into the desk behind him as she cut through the remaining zip ties. Curling off the table was impossible, so instead she rolled off the side. Her knees screamed as she hit uneven floorboards. Another gush of blood slid down into her waistband, warm and sticky and setting an invisible hourglass in motion. She had to get out of here.

"Run, Maeve. Hide if you can." He pressed his hand into his wound, the blood trickling through his fingers. "Because when I find you, my face will be the last thing you see."

Gripping the serrated blade, she pried herself off the floor and lunged for the door. She wrenched it hard enough to break one of the hinges and burst into a star-speckled night.

To find herself in the middle of nowhere, facing off with Kolob Arch.

Chapter Twenty-Seven

He'd been wrong from the beginning.

Callen hadn't gotten more than a few pages into his sister's notebook—a notebook Maeve had supposedly mishandled as a key piece of evidence in Lauren's investigation—before he'd known exactly what kind of threat had taken Maeve. His gut clenched at the sight of the all-too-familiar handwriting within the pages now tossed in the back seat. It'd taken a couple of minutes to remember the language Maeve and Lauren had made up to communicate with each other about things they didn't want his parents to know about, but he was never more grateful to recall it than now. Okay. Now and the time he'd first heard Maeve ask his sister about him. Lauren had written notes from entire conversations with "C," detailing threats he'd made, ramblings about Maeve that led Callen to believe his brother had been watching her for years and indicators of how intense Cieron's obsession had become mixed in with city development notes, sketches made during city planning meetings and phone numbers to follow through on.

His sister's entire life had been detailed in this one notebook. Meetings, contacts, brainstorming.

And the letter to Maeve. One only she would've been

able to decipher if Callen hadn't gone out of his way to crack their code. And the secret Lauren may have been killed for.

"We're going to find her." Tommy Russell had taken one look at the notebook Callen had pulled from his brother's overnight bag, grabbed a handgun and a box of ammunition for himself, and headed for the SUV. There was no arguing with his father to stay behind. Cieron had killed Lauren, had tried to kill Callen and was potentially on his way to killing Maeve. This was a family issue, and family stood together. His father reached across the SUV's center console, squeezing Callen's aching shoulder.

He hadn't realized how tense he'd become until then and tried to breathe through all the possibilities they'd come across once they reached Kolob Arch. Callen still hadn't heard from Simpson or his law enforcement rangers, but he had to believe Maeve would walk out of the park alive. With or without his help. He raced up the one-lane road curling and double-backing through the northwest side of Zion National Park. The mountains demanding attention from each side of the SUV were bigger, the valleys wider, the trees thicker, the drop-offs steeper. Everything tourists loved about the main trails in the park—the red rock cliffs, raging rivers and beautiful, winding views—were more beautiful out here. No longer consolidated to approved hikes and rules within a few square miles, the Kolob Canyons section of the park was solely made of backcountry. With a thousand different places a killer might take a victim. "She has to be there."

"She will be." His father's confidence spread through the interior of the SUV, most of it coming from years of his own military service and no-nonsense parenting. He'd witnessed his three children do the dumbest things of their lives—hurt one another, hurt themselves, take risks that never paid off and more—and yet nothing seemed to faze the man. Tommy held on to the sidearm he'd borrowed from Callen's arsenal like the pro he was. On alert. Ready for anything. It'd been that born and bred confidence his dad carried that'd given Callen the courage to invest in a private security company and become one of its key operators for years, to ask his sister's best friend on their first date after she turned eighteen and then later ask her to marry him. His father had taught him to adapt and endure through good times and bad, and without that influence, Callen wasn't sure where he would be. Who he would be. There wasn't a single gene in Callen's entire DNA he didn't attribute to the man sitting in the passenger seat, and Callen couldn't be more grateful to have his dad here now. "Your instincts are better than you think they are."

The interstate arrowed straight past the Kolob Canyons visitor center, cutting off more than an hour of having to drive north through the park. They would still have to curve south and ditch the SUV to get on to the Kolob Arch trail, and Callen's heart refused to let him forget every minute that slipped through his fingers.

"My instincts were wrong about her." Maeve had never been responsible for compromising Lauren's missing person investigation. She'd never mishandled the evidence that led police to let the case go cold. Cieron. It was all Cieron. Who'd killed their sister, leaving her skeletal remains on that trail. Who'd abducted a forensic analyst to garner Maeve's attention. Who'd zip-tied him to a steering wheel and driven his truck into the Virgin River. His brother had pointed a gun at him and pulled the trigger, intending to get Callen out of the way. All this time he'd fought to keep his family together, and Cieron had been pulling it apart piece by piece. "I gave up on her. Even when she refused to give up on us."

"Yeah. You made a dumb decision, but you're here now. That's what matters. You're fighting for her now, and sooner or later, you're going to have to forgive yourself for those choices." The passenger seat groaned as his dad shifted. Setting his head back against the headrest, Tommy Russell closed his eyes, as though sensing the pain to come. Because there would be pain. There would be blood. And it wouldn't be Maeve's. "All I ask is that you don't forget who you are, son."

Understanding hit, and Callen couldn't hold on to the shallow breath he'd taken as he ripped the steering wheel to the right and pulled to a stop at the Kolob Arch trailhead. Slamming the vehicle into Park, he grabbed his weapon. "You're asking me not to take Cieron down. After everything he's done—not just killing Lauren or Iliana Meyer, but hurting Maeve—you want me to let him walk away?"

"I'm asking you to do your job. You're a protector. You always have been. Don't let all that anger you've been carrying change that." His dad shouldered out of the passenger side and rounded the hood of the SUV, weapon drawn. Headlights cast Tommy's shadow over the trailhead's sign directing hikers into the dark. "Now, stop living in the past and go claim your future."

Determination settled into his bones. And Callen could do nothing but follow. He couldn't make that promise to his dad. If push came to shove, he'd do whatever it took to protect Maeve, including choosing her over his brother. But he had no idea whether it would come to that. Whether he'd even get to her in time.

Directing his flashlight ahead, he picked up the pace, feeling every jolt, every burn in his lungs the closer he drew to the arch. His father kept pace with a few stumbles, but the man had taught his children to keep going, keep pushing. Tommy Russell had never expected anything of his kids without being willing to do what he was asking personally, even well into his sixties, and he wouldn't start now.

"When was the last time you ran six miles, old man?" The uneven terrain and sharp rocks poking through the compacted dirt threatened to trip them up. Callen's heavy panting faded into the surrounding darkness. He could only see the next few steps in front of him, steady on course. He hiked this trail multiple times a week, but the elevation changes were beating on every cell he owned. Or was that the desperation squeezing his chest?

"Is this the fastest you can run?" His dad kept a few paces behind, unknowingly pushing Callen that much harder. "Expected better of a man almost half my age."

A growl resonated from Callen's chest. He pumped his legs, the distance between him and his father growing with each step until Kolob Arch came into view. There weren't any details or colors to pick out against the star-scattered sky, wispy with white clouds. Sweat beaded at his temple as he slowed just before the hill of boulders leading to the arch. The winter temperatures did nothing to bring down his body temperature. There was only one path to neutralize the anxiety crushing through him. She was here. She had to be here. "Where are you, Maeve?"

Movement registered from his left, a split second before a wall of lean muscle slammed into him. The ground rushed up to meet him, and Callen landed on his right side, skidding into a boulder. A fist rocketed into his temple. Once. Twice. Cieron pulled a sidearm from his back waistband, ready to finish what he'd started at the river. "You just couldn't let me have her, could you?"

The cold barrel burned against his temple. Callen's vision wavered, his head pounded, but he managed to get his leg around his brother's chest. "You never deserved her."

A rock slammed into the side of Cieron's head.

The gun discharged mere inches from Callen's right ear. A high-pitched ringing screamed through his head before pain exploded in its place.

His brother twisted toward the source of the rock. And took aim.

It took a moment for Callen to blink away the dizziness accompanied by adrenaline burning through his veins.

"It's not him you want, Cieron." That voice. Her voice. It'd lost some of its strength, but Maeve stood there, one hand limp at her side while the other was clamped against her shirt. Blood-drenched and beautiful. She backed up a couple of steps, as though she had all the time in the world, but Callen recognized the sluggishness in her step. Her body was failing her. Threatening to take her from him all over again. "Come and get me."

Callen put everything he had into pinning his brother to the dirt with that one leg, but his brother was faster. Cieron scrambled out of reach, but Callen wouldn't let him put another hand on Maeve. "You won't get another chance, Cieron. Finish this."

Callen lunged. Kicking off a boulder to his right, he

attacked knee-first. Straight into his brother's chest. The impact knocked Cieron back, and his brother hit the ground. Cieron raised his gun. And pulled the trigger.

The bullet ripped past Callen's ear. Stinging pain chased back the dizziness from the slug to his head. Callen kicked out, his shin connecting with his brother's chest again, and another bullet shot through the night. But his luck wouldn't last. Grabbing Cieron's wrist, he squeezed the tendons in the bastard's hand, forcing him to drop the gun. Metal thudded against the ground.

The distraction cost him.

Cieron struck. His foot collided with Callen's face, and the whole world lit up. Stumbling back, he barely had the sense to stay conscious as his brother closed the distance between them. Callen brought one foot up. Bones collapsed beneath his heel as he kicked Cieron to the ground. Pain messed with his head but provided clarity at the same time. Kept him in the moment. Standing over his brother, Callen took in the blood streaked across Cieron's face. "Why?"

Why kill Lauren? Why cost Maeve her job? Why abduct Iliana Meyer? Why try to kill Callen? Just…why?

"Because I saw her first." A slick smile pulled at one side of Cieron's mouth as he climbed to his feet. His brother stumbled back a step, then righted himself. Spreading his arms wide, Cieron laughed. "But you're the oldest. You always got what you wanted. Isn't that right? You got our parents' praise growing up. You got Lauren's loyalty until the end, when she was going to warn you about me. You got Maeve's devotion even after you destroyed her life. They looked at you like you hung the moon, but I see the truth. You're nothing without them, and I… I just wanted one thing for myself. I wanted Maeve, but you couldn't even let me have that."

"I never wanted this." Footsteps registered in Callen's good ear, coming up the trail. Tommy Russell sounded as though he were going to drop dead, and Maeve… She was hurt, barely able to stand.

Cieron's smile drained. "Yeah, well. For once, I'm going to make sure you don't get what you want this time." His brother spun on his heel, stretching for Maeve.

And Callen didn't hesitate.

Grabbing for the gun between them, he raised it and took aim.

Pulling the trigger.

Chapter Twenty-Eight

She couldn't feel her toes.

Actually, she couldn't feel much of anything with the steady drip in her arm. That was probably the least important thing about waking in the middle of a hospital bed again, but it seemed important.

"You're looking better." Movement slithered into her peripheral vision from beside the bed. It took only a couple of seconds for Callen's features to clear the haze clouding her sense of reality. Those dark eyes settled on her, as though memorizing her all over again. The ends of his hair clung to his nape and curled slightly. He'd showered and changed. Fresh bruises darkened along one side of his face, not yet turning green and yellow. He'd taken quite the beating out there on the trail, but he was still standing.

She couldn't claim the same. "They really should market blood transfusions in the beauty industry. Does wonders for the skin."

His laugh deepened as he ducked his head, but she caught the traces of concern before he could hide them. Of stress and loss. Cieron had killed their sister to keep his secret, and that had to hurt. She'd never had siblings, but there was a new space in her chest she wasn't sure could ever be filled. Cieron had taken on the role of a goofy big brother in her life for years, and now? She didn't know what to think, didn't know how long it would take before the truth settled, but she would help any way she could. She'd do anything for the Russells.

"What's the damage this time?" Maeve peeled the sheets away from her gown—a different one from her last visit—and made out a white layer of gauze stretched over her stomach secured with tape. She was alive. That fact hadn't hit until now. She was alive, they'd recovered Lauren's remains and her killer had been brought to justice. It was everything she'd worked for and more.

"Well, your insurance threatened to stop coverage if you leave the hospital without being officially discharged again, but other than that, it's looking good." He scanned her midsection like he was trying to assure himself she was really here. "You tore through two sutures. One of them was responsible for all the bleeding, but overall, doctors are confident you're going to make it."

"Good." She could almost take a full breath without wanting to pass out. That was a good sign. "I paid extra for gunshot wounds. The least they could do is cover the claim."

"You never told me where you've been all this time. Since you moved out." Callen leaned back in his seat, muscled arms crossing over his broad chest, and hell, she couldn't stop the shooting warmth in her lower belly. He'd always been handsome, but a new appreciation—maybe from almost dying—swept in. "You obviously never made it to Vegas or transferred to the FBI office there. How have you been surviving?"

"Off my dad's life insurance. Hotels here, Airbnbs there." She didn't need to tell him about the nights she'd spent in her car, unless she wanted to hear a lecture about safety and putting herself at risk. "I picked up a couple private investigations. Iliana Meyer was one of them. Her boyfriend… He hired me. I guess Iliana had told him about me from the one case we'd worked together, and he reached out." A wave of sorrow rushed in at the thought of having that conversation. She'd liked Iliana. Might've even been friends with her if their lives had crossed a few more times, but now there was no chance for that. "Has your brother told police where he has her?"

"As far as I know, Cieron isn't cooperating." Callen cut his attention across the room. "My parents have tried to convince him to take a deal to give Iliana's family closure. They hired him an attorney believing there's still a piece of the kid they raised in there, but he's not interested in saving himself. Never has been."

The sensation of blood splattering all over her as Cieron lunged for her prickled across her face and neck. It wasn't there, but she could still feel it. See him drop to his knees. Follow the roll of his eyes into the back of his head. Law enforcement rangers had gotten to them in time, able to drive both her and Cieron down the trail. Saving her life. And his. He'd see the inside of a cell as soon as he was recovered. "And your mom? What does she think of all this?"

"I'm not sure yet. She's not talking much. It's a lot to handle, waiting to find out if your daughter is alive all this time. Even more unnerving to learn one of your other children was responsible for her death. Dad is taking care of her." That same weight resonated in his voice, though he wouldn't admit it. "But Simpson and his rangers found the ranger station he held you in. It's not one we use often, and Cieron seemed to know that. They also found another set of remains. They were soaking in bleach, like Lauren's, presumably to get rid of any DNA, but Dr. Yarrow is confident he'll be able to get an identity in the next couple of days."

Good. That was good. Maeve set her head back against the pillows. And if those remains didn't belong to Iliana Meyer, she would keep searching. She'd hike every mile of Zion if she had to. Because Iliana's boyfriend deserved answers. Closure.

"I'm sorry. I can't imagine how hard this must be for you and your parents." Her hand brushed against her stomach, and she nearly curled in on herself as colors lit up behind her eyes. When she could finally breathe through it, Callen looked as though he was ready to bring down the building to make it stop. "I'm okay."

His gaze snapped to her, the tendons along his neck and across his shoulder bulging with pent-up tension. "You're not okay. Cieron—a man you've cared for and trusted for years—put a bullet in you. He was going to kill you if you hadn't stabbed him first. Don't tell me you're okay, and don't lie to me thinking you need to soften the blow. I know what he's done, and I know who he is. Part of me doesn't want to believe it, but my brother hurt you, Maeve. You don't have a damn thing to be sorry about."

As much as she wanted to believe she wasn't at fault for any of this, she knew the truth. "None of this would've happened if I hadn't lost track of that notebook."

"You didn't." Bending down, Callen collected something from his belongings on the floor and tossed a bright yellow notebook onto the bed.

Not just any yellow notebook. Her entire body shook

as she skimmed her fingers over the pages. "I don't… I don't understand. How do you have that?"

"I found it in Cieron's overnight bag. I don't know why he's held on to it all this time, but it's Lauren's.

"She made notes in it in that stupid language you two made up when you were younger and didn't think anyone else would figure out you borrowed words from every other language out there."

"Some serial offenders like to keep trophies. It reminds them of the high they felt when they killed that victim." Tears burned in her eyes. Stupid pain medications. At what point would she learn not to have these kinds of conversations after almost winding up dead? Maeve let her fingers still on the soft cover. "I never lost the evidence."

Those five words soothed the guilt and the shame that'd been clawing through her for months. Cieron had told her he'd taken the notebook from her hotel room that night, but she wasn't sure if she'd imagined it due to blood loss or if he'd been lying. Though she couldn't imagine why he would.

"Cieron admitted to killing Lauren because she was going to warn you about his intentions." He'd taken on that stillness again, his anger practically vibrating through the whole room. Not for her, but for what she'd been through, she realized. How close she'd come to never walking out of that park alive. "He must've stayed in Springdale to watch the search for her unfold. I'm guessing he didn't expect you to show up to work the case, and he took advantage when he saw the opportunity to compromise the investigation."

"He didn't know about the notebook until I pulled it from Lauren's car. I guess I made it easy for him by not submitting it to the evidence locker that night, but I just wanted… I wanted to have something of hers. Just for a little while, and she carried that damn thing everywhere. It was practically an extension of her." A tremor passed through her hand as she traced a sunflower her best friend had drawn onto the cover. "He told me Lauren had taken notes on things he'd said about me, about you. What he intended to do. I can't imagine he was sober when he admitted to them."

"I've had an old contact of mine go through every back door in the code for my unit's security system. It was never hacked." He tossed his phone onto the end of the bed, face up. "Looks like Cieron was able to guess my app's password, knowing which ones I preferred. It's the same code for my gun safe. From what I can put together, he was able to access my storage unit multiple times by logging into my account, changing the phone number in the settings and moving in and out as he pleased, making sure I never saw the notifications."

"He left that Taser at the riverbank to frame you for Iliana Meyer's disappearance and, in connection, Lauren's." How long had Cieron's game been in play? How many years had she been blind to his obsession and pain? "I'm assuming he was also responsible for locking me in the storage unit?"

"I think he meant to keep you out of the way while he worked another strategy to get me out of the way." Callen cleared his throat. "Didn't work, thanks to you. The fingerprints you ran weren't officially connected to any case, but Springdale PD is in possession of the Taser now. As Dr. Yarrow promised. But since Cieron has been arrested, I'm in the clear."

Silence reigned for a beat. Then two.

"She wrote you a letter." Callen nodded to the notebook. "It's... Now might not be the time to read it, but I couldn't keep it from you. You deserve to know she didn't think the man arrested for your dad's murder was guilty. She believes Cieron may have been involved." The weight of his gaze pressed against her chest. Not suffocating, but grounding. Comfortable and reliable. Just like him. She didn't want to imagine what might've happened if Callen hadn't come for her. If she would end up in that cold basement next to Lauren. And she didn't want to think about Lauren's accusation just yet. "You can take all the time you need or not read it at all, Maeve. I can look into her theory by myself and keep you updated, or we can work together to find the truth. I'll support you in whatever way you decide, but it's your choice."

He was right. She wasn't ready to read Lauren's notebook or consider the man Callen had hunted down and turned over to the police may have been innocent. Not yet. But she would get there. "Does this mean you can take Lauren home?"

"Dr. Yarrow released her remains this morning. My parents wanted to stay until you woke up, but I told them they should go home and make arrangements." He set his elbows on his knees, the picture of ease, but she knew every muscle in his body was honed to confront the next threat at a moment's notice. "They'll have a funeral in a few weeks, when you're strong enough to attend."

"They don't have to do that." She tried to push herself upright. "They've been waiting—"

"And they'll continue to wait until you're well enough to be there. We weren't the only ones to lose Lauren,

Maeve, and I'm sorry if I've made you feel like you didn't deserve to be grieving with us or that you didn't belong with us. I was wrong." Callen grabbed her hand, skimming his thumb across the bruises and scabs already forming across her knuckles. "From the very beginning, I needed someone to blame, and I took my anger out on you because I think I convinced myself if I could survive losing you, I could survive losing Lauren a little easier."

He stared at their intertwined hands. "It was stupid, but I made it happen. I made myself suffer in hopes of callusing some part of me, but you just wouldn't let me go, and you'll never know how grateful I am that you didn't stop fighting for my family." Raising her hand to his mouth, he planted a kiss in the center of her palm. "None of this was your fault, and I will spend the rest of my life reminding you of that if that's what you need."

"I might not need daily reminders, but it's nice to know you're committed to your cause." She was getting tired again, the pressure and weight of the past year draining her in increments. It would take longer than a few days to come to terms with what had happened—who had paid with their lives—but for the first time in a long time, she had hope for the future.

A smile tugged at only half his mouth as he brought his free hand up, pressing it into her palm. Something warm pressed into her skin. "Rangers recovered one of my tactical blades from that ranger station, covered in Cieron's blood. Looked like someone stabbed him."

"He tried to stab me first." Okay. She hadn't meant to get so defensive, but it was the truth.

"You're amazing. You know that, don't you? And I am utterly and completely unworthy of you in every way."

Callen slid one hand from hers, revealing the engagement ring that used to sit on her ring finger in the palm of her hand. "I love you, Maeve. I've been in love with you since our first date. I don't know what our future holds right now in terms of careers and where to live and everything else, but this past year of my life has been empty and cold and hollow because you haven't been in it, and I never want to go through that again. I want you. If you'll have me."

"I love you, too. And I'll make it easy for you. I'm jobless and homeless, so I'll pretty much follow you anywhere." Maeve couldn't hold her smile as she closed her hand over the ring and leaned forward, pressing on the new sutures to reach him, but Callen closed the distance between them first. His mouth was on hers in an instant, her ring sheltered between them. "So long as you remember you were always worthy, Ranger Russell."

"Deal, Agent Perry." He smiled against her mouth as he set the ring onto her finger. "Forever."

* * * * *